DISABILITY

DISABILITY

CRIS MAZZA

Beverly,
Thanks for coming
to see me in
Des Moines!
Best,
C. Mazza

FC2
NORMAL/TALLAHASSEE

Published by FC2 with support provided by Florida State University, the
Publications Unit of the Department of English at Illinois State University,
the Florida Arts Council of the Florida Division of Cultural Affairs, and the
National Endowment for the Arts.

Address all inquiries to: Fiction Collective Two, Florida State University,
c/o English Department, Tallahassee, FL 32306-1580

ISBN: Paper, 1-57366-121-X

Library of Congress Cataloging-in-Publication Data
Mazza, Cris.
 Disability / by Cris Mazza.
    p. cm.
 ISBN 1-57366-121-X
 1. Nurses' aides—Fiction. 2. Children with disabilities—Fiction. 3.
Children—Hospitals—Fiction. 4. Lesbian mothers—Fiction. I. Title.
 PS3563.A988D57 2005
 813'.54—dc22
                        2004027535

Cover Design: Lou Robinson
Book Design: Jeremiah Stanley and Tara Reeser

Produced and printed in the United States of America
Printed on recycled paper with soy ink

NATIONAL
ENDOWMENT
FOR THE ARTS

Acknowledgements made to the following publications in
which portions of this novel first appeared:

Water~Stone for portions of chapter 1 and 3,
titled "Therapeutic"

Jabberwock for portions of chapter 1 and 3,
titled "Therapeutic"

In memory of
Marie Mazza
1924-2004
Ward of the State of California 1937-2004

1.

The funk is always penetrated & acknowledged 1st. Hot dogs & mashed potatoes & wet carpet & industrial disinfectant & plastic toys & usually pee & sometimes poop. Hardly noticeable to Teri anymore *except* during that 1st stride through the glass door at the end of the hall. Like entering an aquarium from 1 end — a heavy piece of glass that swings out then re-seals. The interior air like water that doesn't escape & stays shaped like a long rectangular box circulated through a filter of some sort but is never exchanged w/ the atmosphere outside.

State ward for profoundly retarded severely disabled children — not a castle on an endless lawn but a contracted-out portion of a suburban convalescent hospital 2/3 still geriatric the last long wing now housing young & juvenile morons & idiots. Walls painted sky blue w/ friendly fluffy clouds. Filtered sun comes through the glass doors to warm the 1st few feet of sea blue pee & poop & sometimes vomit-stained carpet.

After high school graduation 12 or 13 years ago Teri's part-time job as a hospital housekeeper became geriatric nurse-aide w/o a raise in minimum-wage pay. Since then a lot of changes like w/o consent impregnated w/ a child who stuck around 8 years more or less then chose to live w/ the source of sperm — but the job in 1 form or another remains & remains part-time. 3 years ago the half-empty last wing was not recarpeted but cleaned & painted & cribs purchased then idiots brought in by ambulance 1 by 1. Idiot is a medical term. There are other medical terms on their charts — syndromes disorders palsies.

Every 2 rooms share a bathroom every bathroom has a toilet & sink & mirror no tub. A tangled ball of sheets & towels on the floor at the start of every afternoon shift left by the AM aides. Cows who work full time from 7 to 4 then go bowling or to bingo either waiting for their navy husbands to come home from westpac or spending weekends washing motorcycle grease from garage jumpsuits. At work watch soaps & game shows on the B&W TVs which every room in the hospital has 1 of. Teri changes both her TVs to reruns of *Rawhide* then *Leave it to Beaver* then *I Love Lucy* then *Rockford Files* then *Mary Tyler Moore* then *Unsolved Mysteries*. 4 hours of TV shift over. Every bed changed every child diapered twice or more *p.r.n.* every stomach filled every poopy diaper rinsed before being flung down the chute every lunch-crusted t-shirt peeled away & likewise down the chute w/ the sheets & towels. Potatoes creamed peas dried milk pureed meat washed from creases in necks navels & crotches *s.o.s.* Skin lotioned & powdered. Arms & legs wrestled into clean t-shirt or nightgown or footed pjs then restrained or otherwise strapped in bed w/ rail up & blanket available for night shift to repeatedly replace over twisting or deathly still body. Shift over.

But it's also 4 hours 5 days a week w/ Danny. He's 9/yrs wears diapers & creeps around on his stomach on the floor. Once they nicknamed him snake but it didn't stick there's no scary ominous peril when you see him slithering. He's had a few other nicknames too — *poopbutt* & *Little Man* & *girl* b/c he's pretty & he screams but mostly he's *scooterboy*. He has crossed eyes & legs that look like twisted pipecleaners & brown spots on his crooked teeth & long blond curls & a little blue wheelchair. He spends a lot of time screeching while strapped in the wheelchair w/ the wheels locked. He also has braces & spends a lot of time screaming while wearing those too. On the floor w/ legs free he laughs & chortles & rubs his cheek against people's ankles then bats a big rubber ball watches it go & chases it traveling arm over arm faster than you'd think possible.

4 pieces of sliced hot dog & 3 green beans huddle at the bottom of the toilet where someone rinsed a bib after lunch. *Toilets Are Not Trash Cans* the sign above the tank says so it will be flushed after Teri pees or as soon as she checks which of her 8 kids have pooped since the AM shift left or had already pooped before that but the cow decided not to delay clocking out thinking *let the PM part-timers do it*. 3 times she's passed up a move to the AM full time shift to continue earning unreported cash in the morning mowing lawns & trimming bushes. The year-round California sun is hell on her face which stays white around the eyes from sunglasses & elsewhere growing leathery. Her workmate of 2 years & new roommate of 2 months Cleo uses Oil of Olay — Teri's seen it in the bathroom but hasn't asked Cleo what made her think to plan ahead at 22/yrs. Cleo's station is the 2 rooms across the hall w/ 8 slightly younger kids who are slightly smaller than Teri's even though Cleo's not

smaller. Cleo lucked-out & got group 2 — not the babies but next group up. Teri still has group 3 which includes Cheryl 14/ yrs & she plays w/ her yellowish diarrhea which she has every day even though she eats a chopped not pureed diet.

But Teri also has Danny. Experimenting w/ tongue & teeth he makes sounds that are almost words & has enough brain to be capable of boredom unless entertained & can't be mollified w/ a blabbering TV or wind-up musical crib ornament — he needs action & adventure a real boy a boy's boy.

The TV in the room on the right hasn't been changed yet — the *Jeopardy* song counting down — in the other room Clint Eastwood as Rowdy in *Rawhide* talks quiet sense before he punches someone out. She pees & flushes & is washing her hands when Cleo slips silently on crepe soles into the bathroom puts her hands on Teri's shoulders turns her around leans against Teri's forehead w/ her own — noses squished together & Cleo's mouth talking w/ lips touching Teri's lips. "He's here."

"What's he like?"

"His pants make whizzy sounds. He's calling a meeting right now."

"We haven't changed anyone yet."

"*You* haven't. Mine're done." Cleo picks up the bundle of linen. "I'll take these out for you. They're not your *clean* ones are they?"

"Har-de-har. I'll be right there. I'm going to do Danny first."

She sings *There was a crooked man who walked a crooked mile* while loosening the strings on the heavy white shoes attached to the ends of his hip-to-ankle stainless steel & soft leather w/ sheepskin padding braces. If he knows the braces are being readied he'll curl his foot like a fist & nothing will fit —

the shoe impossible to tie the brace impossible to lock into place. So after the braces are gaping open she changes his diaper just wet. Still singing now also tickling his tummy kneels astride his no bigger than a 4-yr-old body her back to his face so he pounds on her back w/ his strong hand & laughs not realizing she's pulling the braces closer. Tickling his foot relaxing it slipping it into the shoe while her finger continues to tickle her voice continues to sing. At the last second her finger flicks his toes straight & the shoe is on quickly laced. His face puckers but a wiggling finger into his armpit makes him giggle & forget to scream so the other foot relaxes too. Once the shoes are on the rest is easy except the force required to lock the metal in place so his legs are straight & knees & feet actually face forward.

She holds his hands & stands him up. "Dance with me, Little Man." 1 of his legs is shorter but no provision built into the bottom of the shoe so he only stands on 1 foot unless she tips him. His face getting ready to scream but obviously also wondering if he should laugh. But Danny's no fool — doesn't want to be immobile & the scream will win out after Teri has to leave him to change the other kids. A towel for a rope she ties his straightened body to a wide scooter-board w/ small wheels so he can crawl w/ the same arm over arm motion. But it's more difficult to crawl when he's on the scooter not the same leverage for his arms 2 inches higher off the carpet. He hits the ball & stares cross-eyed after it then bends face to the floor to dig in & chase it.

Cleo & the 6 other PM aides are already in the new therapy room at the end of the ward sitting on round bolsters or pillows on thick floor mats. But no one's in the lone granny-like rocking chair which is usually in Teri's room across the hall but someone has moved it here & it's placed like a lectern facing the circle of girls on the mats. Teri sits beside Cleo sitting alone upright on the edge of the waterbed that butts up against the mats. The other aides talk about their new fall schedules at college & new men they've been seeing & cars they're thinking of buying & where they've found hospital smocks half price & how the AM shift has powdered half the kids instead of changing them & the 17-yr-old boy in group 8 was left in bed all day & is masturbating.

The hinges creak & the new administrator of some sort squeezes himself through the barely opened door. Not tall & slightly doughy w/ powder blue & white checked shirt. Once inside he pushes the door all the way open & leaves it. "What do you think of the new room?" A peculiarly high voice sweet & mellow. Behind him Danny pulls himself into view & stares into the room then turns his head & closes his eyes w/ effort. Swivels & drags the scooter holding his body off the hall carpet & onto the linoleum floor.

"As you read in the memos last week, I'm the new program director for the children on this ward." A black organizational notebook held under 1 arm like a clutch purse. Pasty skin hasn't seen the sun in maybe forever & looks like he'd be clammy to the touch. "My name is Frank Bishop, and here on the ward I'll ask you to play a little game called Frank and Earnest. I'll, of course, be Frank, and you'll be Earnest." No one laughs & it looks like instead of blushing he'll only get a thready spiderweb of veins on his cheeks if anyone wanted to be close enough to look. "Anyway, the state has determined that these children warrant more than basic care. Their conditions are all being reviewed by physical and occupational therapists to plot their individual programs." Eye sockets that look too small being stretched as wide as they go for washed-out blue eyes to be able to see through. Hair drained of color or too short & neatly combed to tell. "Those deemed suitable for therapy will have, in their charts, a specific goal and set of instructions for therapy, and the nurse-aides, both morning and afternoon shifts, will do a daily therapy session with each child, charting results and progress at least once a week. And let me tell you in advance, we've only been preliminarily assessed. The more progress the state sees, the more money will be allocated when the programs are reassessed." Teri waits to see if a dark sweat spot will start to grow where the notebook is still pressed into his armpit creasing the fresh shirt. He's right behind the rocking chair & Danny's behind him until he comes around & sits in the chair & crosses his legs. Cleo was right his pants make a zippery sound b/c they're fat-ribbed corduroy. Notebook now resting on his knees he opens it & shuffles through papers. Employee schedules lists of residents state assessment results therapy consultant phone numbers therapy schedules. Assembled typed arranged graphed charted. Each aide receives a schedule for her group those days & hours they are to use the therapy room & the rest of the time therapy is to take place in their own rooms.

"Individual therapy programs are being placed into each of the patients' charts" he repeats. Lifting 1 leg to cross it over the other the corduroy zips & the notebook tilts almost dumping many multi-colored sheets on the floor but 1 hand slaps down like squashing a fly & catches everything in place. "There's fine motor and gross motor, tactile awareness, aural awareness, we have a few children who'll do colors, plus the occupational therapies, chewing, swallowing, toilet training, etcetera. And physical goals: rolling over, clapping, bending knees, crawling."

"No playing baseball?" Cleo asks w/ hand raised but she speaks simultaneously w/o being called on. "No soccer or bicycles?" Teri crashes backwards onto the waterbed making waves that cause Cleo's head to bob. Many of the aides laugh a sound like spitting or sneezing. Danny's no longer in danger w/ fingers no longer too close to the rocking runners of the wooden chair — he's gone under the circular table that has cut-out slots for wheeling a kid close enough so the table surface comes around the sides of a wheelchair — & he's out the other side trying to reach a blue plastic crate full of multicolored plastic toys inches too high on a shelf & he shrieks in guileless frustration. He does manage to grab a stuffed bunny obviously donated 2nd hand & the victim of a thousand trips through the washing machine. It doesn't go very far when he bats it like a ball.

Bishop says "You'll be called therapy aides now. The nurse is still in charge of their basic health and you'll do those duties as before and follow any instructions she gives you. But we're going beyond basic care now."

"Are we getting paid more?" someone asks. The someone wasn't Cleo who's now flat on her back beside Teri. The someone also wasn't Teri who's busy using her hips to help Cleo keep the waves moving on the waterbed.

"You'll still be working the same number of hours, so ...."

"*No*, in other words" Cleo says to the blue ceiling.

"You're employees of this hospital, and the hospital has a contract to maintain this ward. That includes all the types of care the state decides are mandatory."

Danny shrieks higher shriller b/c the bunny's faded floppy ears are wedged under 1 of his wheels & he can't move forward or back.

"So when're we supposed to make beds, change kids, and feed? It takes me two hours to feed mine." So says the baby-group aide. Once Teri had come in on a day off to do the babies when the regular aide was sick they do take forfuckingever to feed — they have no concept of eating it runs out of their mouths & down their necks. Danny now screaming nonstop contorts & twists his body until he manages to roll to his back like a turtle 4 wheels up in the air. He's in a patch of sun laid across the linoleum by the sliding glass door that opens to a patio & lawn & unused playground.

Bishop glances at Danny while saying maybe as loud as his delicate voice can get "I believe your group has the least time-consuming therapy. Mostly aural and tactile awareness. And I believe chewing and swallowing will be *part* of their programs as well."

They all begin talking between Danny's shrieks as his vocalizations turn rhythmic gathering air screeching gathering air & grinning roguishly while he rests.

"Where'd you work before this?"

"I was an aide like you, ten years at a home for retarded adults."

"So you hit the administrative big time?" Cleo's voice crisp like snapping clean sheets before they float down onto the mattress.

"Hey!" someone interrupts. "I've got a hydrocephalic who only has a brain stem."

"Each child has been *assessed*. Not all of them will get therapy."

"What about the boardboy?" Cleo's voice dry like cutting paper w/ an arm across her eyes the other across her nose & mouth still thrusting hips to make the waterbed slosh higher.

Looking sideways Teri can recognize Cleo's smile even w/ most of her face covered. Danny's not boardboy but scooterboy. He plays patty-cake which Teri taught him last year palm of his good hand beating the back of his weak hand.

"I expect there'll be many questions as you read the programs, so it'll probably be best for me to answer specific concerns as they come up." Bishop rocks forward & uncrosses his legs then presses his knees together to make a flat surface & pats the papers in the notebook straight.

"Hey, can we go?" Cleo abruptly sits upright. "If I don't get enough diapers and sheets when the laundry comes down, someone'll be sleeping in a peepool."

Now some color in his face Bishop's cheeks are pinkish but his lips thin & bloodless. Before he says anything everyone gets up & leaves anyway b/c the afternoon cart full of diapers towels & sheets is waiting at the nurse's station & it's a free-for-all to get as much linen as you can. *Armed for battle against bodily fluids* Cleo calls it wheeling her own tray table piled w/ stiff white diapers & thin white towels & even thinner white sheets back to her rooms. Teri has an equal hog's portion & they'll share later on if either has a catastrophe of spilled food vomit mucus urine or feces. They talk almost constantly at work *about* work but no rap sessions around the living room of the little house & no talk ever about what Cleo does all day besides these 4 hours of part-time bottom-of-the-food-chain work nor about Teri's former daughter. Who's to say Teri didn't deserve what she got — not from the sperm donor but from the child who became priceless only after she was gone. Maybe Teri didn't deserve the girl in the 1st place since she's so concerned *now* about who's telling her to do what w/ someone else's abandoned defective kids but she had never once thought to worry that the healthy whole girl she carried to term would choose not to have a mother.

Two.

There isn't any question in Cleo's mind that she'll be part of a united front standing on the *reality* side of the therapy question. They may make the lowest possible wage, working routinely up to their elbows in the most basic functions of life — food in one end, waste out the other — but they aren't *stupid*, after all. The money spent for therapists and consultants could be buying more diapers made out of something besides corrugated sandpaper, sheets you can't see through, and soap that doesn't leave skin like a weathered board. Not to mention shampoo, toothpaste, hand cream — all of which she and Teri either pilfer from the supply closet or outright steal from sleeping geriatric patients — and food that doesn't all taste like it comes from the same vat of pasteurized slop. She and Teri have their shit together, their timing down pat, their kids the best tended and cleanest, their war against the indolent a.m. full-timers making the most progress. Teri is her comrade in this four-hour-per-day front-line skirmish. The other twenty hours a day, she's barely thought about whether or not Teri should have a place there.

Cleo wouldn't even be rooming with Teri if Windy had said yes to living together. She used to be Wendy but said it was *too* something and changed it, checkbook, credit cards, driver's license, everything, when she landed her late-afternoon FM DJ gig, almost exactly the same four hours Cleo's here, which is why Cleo looked for a job with this shift. She's hardly ever heard Windy's show — the tacky hospital radios won't pick up an alternative cable station. Maybe someday she'll become the kind of lover Windy will commit to, but so far Windy said no living together and didn't say why. So Cleo has her own room in Teri's little house that sits in the backyard of someone else's house, except the nights she sometimes spends at Windy's after one of their tempestuous dates. Tempestuous means *good*. A raw, inflamed, buzzing, roller coaster ride of adrenalin, dirty dancing together in a skinhead bar or fingering each other at the end of the pier when the tide is high and the waves crash up and over them. And doing it again at home, or sometimes in the car — it took *hours* to lick the salt and sand from every inch of skin, every crevice. When Windy calls for a date, she says, "I got a girl-boner throbbing for you, sweetie, wash off the shithouse and let's go *in* to eat."

The shithouse — the hospital. She and Windy never talk about the contorted, twisted kids, groaning like cattle for their dinners, smiling and drooling, sweating in soiled sheets when she comes in for her afternoon shift. Teri is usually already here, having come directly from her last lawn-mowing customer, faded blond hair in a stub ponytail, two escaped tendrils hanging on either side of her eyes as she slaps a wet diaper into the laundry chute and looks up with a smile on only one side of her face, grinning crow's feet that say *can you believe what we* DO? Together they take Danny's laundry home each week, so the new t-shirts and jeans they buy him won't get lost in the hospital laundry, or stolen or given to some other aide's favorite. Danny is in Teri's group, but they share him, so they also share Jon, who is officially Cleo's, the boardboy. He'd been the start of their first argument. Cleo, forcing a thick diaper between Jon's rigid legs, no bigger around than her own wrist, about two inches of sunlight between them, never more, never less. Teri had paused in the doorway, watching Cleo, a trickle of pureed spinach down the front of her smock where the spoon had tipped on its way to someone's mouth.

"I kind of wondered," Teri had said slowly, probably shy about asking a lame question. "I mean ... can I ask you a personal question?"

"Shoot," Cleo had said, bracing herself. Cleo doesn't hang much with breeders, but Teri's her *compatriot* — each racing to whip 64 hospital corners on eight beds before the other, looting extra diapers from any aide who didn't hide hers while taking a cigarette break, coaxing Cleo to try a spoonful of the special cheese mashed potatoes the kitchen put on the trays once a week as a treat.

"How do you feel seeing all these ... um, penises?"

"How do I *feel*? You mean, like ...." Then the geyser went off. "Why not just ask me your *real* question, Teri? How do I feel seeing all these *cunts*? Maybe you're worried I might be a little too excited changing the *girls'* diapers?" All the while she was pinning the diaper, easing Jon's pants up, spreading a clean quilt his mother had made onto his beanbag, then laying him there, like a branch.

Teri backed up out of the doorway into the hall, fingering her short ponytail. "That's not what I meant."

"Then why did you *ask*?" She smeared a blob of cream between her hands, pushed the excess up her arms, then used fingertips, thumbs and both palms to stroke lotion across Jon's forehead, across his cheeks and the corners of his nose where the skin was patched with red and rough scales.

"Let's just drop it," Teri said, picking at some dried crusty stuff on her jeans. "I thought we could be open with each other."

"We can be open. I go for girls. If you were curious about *that* I'd understand. Shit, Teri, we've given Danny a bath together. Do you think I look at his wanger and think, whew, thank god I'm a lezzie?" She'd whisked a dirty sheet off the closest bed and used it to make a mummy of Jon's wet, yellow diaper.

"I'm sorry, but I think it's a reasonable thing to be curious about — do you think men are repulsive?"

"Do you think women are?"

"I *am* a woman, so it's different."

"I think straight women *do* think women are repulsive. Don't you think that's weird — grossed out by your own self?" Cleo pushed past Teri in the doorway to send the armload down the chute.

"Not grossed out, just not turned on."

Back to spreading a clean sheet on the bare mattress. "And can't that be what *I* feel when I change a boy's diaper?"

"How about a man's diaper?"

Cleo decided it had gone on long enough. Cleo decided to laugh. "Sweetheart, that should gross *anyone* out. You and I just happen to have iron-clad balls."

Teri had smiled her half-face smile, smoothing one loose wisp of hair behind her ear three times in succession, but it always fell right back down. The same half-face smile as when they'd looked at each other after Bishop's introduction-to-therapy meeting — no need to speak — *this is a crock* quivering on the hard white ridges of Teri's familiar trying-not-to-laugh-out-loud face.

3.

Each aide has 2 rooms connected by a bathroom 4 kids to each room. Teri & Cleo across the hall from each other. If they go room to bathroom to room to hall to room they're going in complete circles & only see each other if they happen to be crossing room to room via the hall at the same time or if they both have dirty diapers to sling down the laundry chute simultaneously. They're lucky since the laundry chute is right beside the door to 1 of Cleo's rooms so they don't have to keep a pile of soiled diapers on the floor in the bathroom waiting for a trip down the hall to the laundry chute. Each diaper & each sheet & each towel can have its own trip to the chute. They talk while they're working — wherever they are in the bathroom or either room their voices meeting out in the hall even when they're not. Talk about what new evidence of AM cow laziness was hidden where in which room. Danny has learned his shrill & high angry parrot shriek is very effective for getting attention

since it's difficult to talk through it. Smiling as he screams &
showing his crooked brown-spotted teeth behind his scarlet
red lips. On his back again braces locked scooterboard attached
to his torso w/ his good hand he spins a wheel over & over then
righting himself faster than any turtle would be able when Teri
says "Here's your ball, go get it." The daily thuds of Troy's
head getting louder right on schedule.

Troy crawls like a frog — hands then haunches hands
then haunches. Now his aide follows behind him herself on
hands & knees holding onto his ankles only allowing him to
move forward if he moves 1 knee 1st then the other. Crawling
like a baby is a precursor to walking — it has to be 1 leg then
the other not both legs at once like hopping so no frog-crawl-
ing allowed. He doesn't like it & stops — refusing to try —
banging his football helmeted head against the wall or floor.
Up & down the hall 1 time before the dinner carts arrive. Head
pounding gets louder as they approach fading again as they
ever so slowly make their way back down the hall. The only
freedom Troy gets but he's got to do it 1 knee 1st & then the
other like a real baby. Troy is 8.

A recent transfer into Cleo's group Angela is 80 pounds
of deadweight 16/yrs old. She can move her head — turn & tip
back & can open her mouth which makes a sound like *Ahhh*.
She has a very low voice. She can smile but her body can't
move not her arms not her legs. She can arch her back. It's not
paralysis but rigidity caused by cerebral palsy. She's not spastic
— the spastic kids never stop moving fluttering jittering can't
control where their hands fly. Angela just the opposite takes 2
to lift & swing her onto the bed at night & back off the bed to
her sheet-covered beanbag in the morning. The B&W TV on in
front of her all day but does she watch it?

"What if Angela is normal inside?" Teri asks. "What if she understands everything? What if she's got normal intelligence but can't do anything about it?"

"God."

Together 1 holding ankles the other lifting her shoulders they heave Angela onto the bed. Even w/ 2 they have to use momentum & swing her like a sack of grain into position. She flops onto the bed & usually laughs. Tonight they're out of position not centered beside the bed & Angela's head hits the nightstand as her body lands on the mattress. Angela's eyes & mouth open round & she bawls *Ahhhh* but w/o the smile that's there when she makes the same sound b/c food carts are parked in the hall & the aroma of some kind of stew is wafting into the air that usually smells of too many other things as well.

"I'm so sorry, Angie." Cleo gently smoothing the hair from Angela's brow while kneeling to tuck in the sheet then puts a big stuffed elephant old & donated from someone who didn't need it any longer between Angela's scissor tight legs to keep them apart & prevent pressure sores. Another smaller stuffed bear so old it hasn't any eyes & has faded to the color of oatmeal tucked under Angela's arm but not for the same reason.

"I'm supposed to have *little* ones. They're getting the groups mixed up" Cleo says. Angela still looking up at them the TV still on & only 6 o'clock.

"So why'd you get her?"

"She doesn't have therapy. Six of mine do — they're trying to make it even so they put Karl in group six. Big difference, I still have five with therapy. Group four only has *three* and the babies have none. Lucky dogs."

"Maybe they have to be able to sit in a wheelchair to rate getting it." Teri turns off the TV flickering blue light on Angela's pale white face.

"Jon don't sit in no wheelchair."

"*He* gets therapy? Why?"

"Hey, you tell me!" Cleo pushes a tray table piled w/ empty rattling dinner dishes into the hall then returns w/ a damp towel to clean a trail of droplets of pureed spinach from the floor. "None of this crap is going to do *any* of 'em any good, Jon may as well get his share of the pie while it lasts, right? As soon as there's no result, the program will be long gone, and the money with it."

"Who's *getting* all this mythical money, anyway?"

"How d'you think they pay all the therapists and Sister Bishop? And I guess there's some new equipment in that room they fixed up."

Teri presses a hand low on the small of her back & arches slow against the pressure. "Bishop is coming to watch the fine motor therapy tomorrow — you have anyone in that?"

"Yeah, Glen!"

Shrieking laughter turn their backs & leave Angie w/ her blind stuffed bear to wait until she falls asleep & no one will come back until the 9 PM diaper check but Teri & Cleo have to clock out by 8:08 no overtime is authorized.

But 1st they do charts together up at the nurse's station where a few bigger kids are still parked in food-crusted wheelchairs. You've got to have some kind of spine & the necessary muscle control to sit upright — what a baby acquires about 6 or 8 months — to sit in a wheelchair. Otherwise there are positioning chairs that look like narrow wooden coffins set upright at an angle w/ a bench seat so you're not standing but sitting in the lidless coffin looking out. The whole thing on a platform w/ wheels so a perfectly floppy kid or one that would tip over or melt into a puddle w/o restraints can sort of sit up w/ the side edges of the box & the 45-degree angle of the back making gravity to help hold him in place. But of course to sit anywhere you have to bend at the waist far enough to make your butt into something to sit *on*.

Every night everyone writes *diapered p.r.n.* in green ink & the charts mount up in boxes in the basement w/ the records of exactly when each b.m. occurred & if a suppository was required & weekly temps & in some cases daily measurements of how much food actually made it to the stomach b/c many of the kids have no idea how to swallow & it's not feasible to tube feed. As a treat some bigger kids are allowed to stay up during charting & hang out at the nurse's station but their aides will have to get them in bed before clocking out. They sit in regular recycled hospital-owned wheelchairs w/ their names written in big sloppy felt tip on the backs & their wheels locked although they are unable to move the chairs by themselves unless they get a hold of the handrail that lines every hall but then more than likely they'll pull the whole chair over before getting it to actually roll anywhere. Danny's chair is like new & not standard hospital stock but bright blue & measured to fit him w/ shiny chrome arms & wheels. He has parents — name & address in his chart — who bought the chair but seldom if ever come to visit. Teri thinks she might've seen his mother once but it really could've been anyone walking down the hall w/ a box of new stuffed animals not looking into any of the rooms not even his but that's where the box was left. Teri wipes the chair clean every night after Danny's in bed which is where he is now although still making his parrot shriek from his room b/c w/o

fail Teri will come back to see him 1 more time before she leaves
& will sing him a goodnight song which makes him shriek again
louder when she does leave.

Everyone will be in bed by 7:45 but now like blobs of
Play-Doh slouched over & no eye contact — legs all wizened
useless gnarled sticks but an arm as though a life of its own
comes reaching out & grabs anything in its path & *everything*
in its path just happens to be crotch or ass level on an aide or
nurse standing there.

"Stephen's trying to cop a feel again" someone announces
jumping sideways to avoid the slothlike hand moving like ra-
dar searching for something to hold. Stephen grins & chuckles
a low sound like a calf whenever an aide squeals.

Teri grunts. "God, just ignore it, he's not *hitting* on anyone. It barely takes a brain *stem* to jack your*self* off, but it
takes *some* grey matter to imagine that touching someone else
with your *hand* will be a turn-on."

"I don't know" Cleo demurs. "Windy's almost a genius,
and she jacks off to beat the band. Excuse the pun."

"You call it *jacking off?*"

"Yeah, what else am I going to call it?"

"Well, *jacking off* implies ... well, like a jack *handle* ...
you know, isn't the idea like a fist holding a *handle* ...?"

"Go on, I'm enjoying this." Cleo smiles as she writes *good
appetite seems cheerful* in Angela's chart.

"I'm just saying there's got to be different terminology
for women."

"And you hoped I'd have a list for you? Like filleting the
fish? Clawing the clam?"

"Well ... whatever ..." Teri claps a chart onto her finished pile. "Anyway grabbing himself may be instinctive, but

to suppose for even a second that Stephen's formed this *idea* that he'd like to touch a girl ... it's ludicrous."

"So, we can add sex therapy to his program to improve his intentions." Cleo signs her name like a green childish scribble that no one will ever be able to read. Blue ink for AM shift green for PM & red for nights. "Besides, this is almost a contradiction to what you were saying last week."

"What did I say?"

"You know, what if some of the kids are gay?"

"I didn't think you heard me."

"I was ignoring you."

Teri opens Danny's chart & writes *1/2 hour in leg-extension braces w/o crying.* "I just thought — shouldn't the morons of any population be a representation of the whole population? And don't we have about the right percentage of each race? Except no Asians. I wonder why not?"

"Maybe they keep their morons home." Cleo scratches the corner of her eye w/ 1 clear-polish painted fingernail. "They prefer to change their own diapers and spoonfeed their own homemade puree then put them in the playpen, every day for 25 years. Only a quarter decade changing diapers and feeding puree. Piece of cake."

"Why 25?"

"They don't live much past that. But hey, that's why this therapy is so damn crucial! Cram in as much as possible during the short time they have, it's important so they can live productive, *independent* lives after they leave here!"

"Or die trying."

"Touché, baby."

Teri watches Cleo writing *pressure wound dressing changed p.r.n.* in Jon's chart. This is the 3rd day in a row that

Cleo has put a tiny green dot of ink on top of the gauze of Jon's last dressing change at around 6 or 6:30 w/ Teri as a witness as eventual proof that the AM shift cow never changes the bandage b/c so far each time the green spot has still been there at 4 PM the next day when they get to work.

"So you don't think this therapy will do *any* of them *any* good?"

"Only by luck. And only if anyone knew what they were doing when they wrote the program in the first place. Just take a look and see what they expect *yours* to do."

"I'm going to say goodnight to Danny, then it'll be time to clock out."

Now every time Teri makes this walk down the hall before departing for home she remembers & reruns an incident that happened a month ago. Not replaying it differently but exactly how it had happened because the ending turned out all right but she has to remind herself what revelation it held for her. It was the time she'd forgotten to safety-pin Danny's pajama top to the bottoms so there would be no way for him to pull up the shirt & get his hand into his diaper. Or maybe there hadn't been any extra pins hanging from the hem of her smock so she just hadn't bothered. She'd dipped through the open doorway & smelled it knowing he needed to be changed & even that soon considered turning around & clocking out as though she hadn't made the extra return goodnight trip to his room & therefore couldn't possibly *know* there was 1 more b.m. to add to his chart. But it was worse than that. He'd smeared it on the bars of his crib & on the wall & even on the white safety-net stretched over the top of the crib that keeps him from climbing out even though he wouldn't be able to stand let alone lift either leg over the rail — it's just in case. 7:55 PM

& she could've legally clocked out 3 minutes ago & still count as 8. The night aide would've found him by 9 or 10 at the latest he'd only have to stay there surrounded by his shit for an hour maybe 2. It was his own fault after all maybe it would teach him not to do it again whereas if he got to get up now & have a game being driven down the hall bare-assed naked in a showerchair to the walk-in shower where he'd chortle as she hosed him off with gentle warm water he'd be tempted to do it again every night wouldn't he? But falling asleep with the smell of his shit inescapable would he dream fetid dreams & wake in fevered nightmarish terror & no mother there to soothe his fears to stroke his head shit-caked hair & all. A mother would. If he had a mother she would. He does have a mother at least an address in his chart. & Teri *is* a mother. Had been. & until *that* particular moment in Danny's reeking room she'd presumed she *could've* been a good mother not *t.i.d.* or *p.r.n.* but a blithe 24/hr shift w/o clock-watching if the Y chromosome had left her *alone* — if he'd given her more $ instead of mandates & orders so she wouldn't've had to endure the sick actually dying baby-sitter roommate. Or even if the volunteer sperm benefactor had given her no $ at all so she wouldn't've had to grant him the weekend custodial visits which turned into whole weeks until the little girl insisted she go to Texas with the man who'd furnished half her DNA & she didn't come back. *I have more friends here* she said *I have* COUSINS! Related by an ejaculation. *So let me come there* but the phone went dead & no letters came. Which shows what kind of mother Teri really was — she never followed she never searched never vowed to never give up like TV mothers do. She wrote & called & waited & faithfully returned to the hospital for 4 hours every day every day every day — at that time as a geriatric aide taking ancient dry bodies to the shower in the vinyl showerchair — till the call came a year or 2 later her little girl saying *don't call or write anymore or try to visit and don't try to pull anything legal or I'll get a divorce then it'll all come out in court what you did.* & not even enough mother-guilt to know what it was she'd done — that's the kind of mother she'd turned out to be. *What you did* the girl had said not *what you didn't do* which makes no sense. It doesn't matter. The further measure of her unfitness as a mother probably that she never *did* pull anything legal or even try. The girl now 12 proving right in the end.

So she had stayed to 8:30 cleaning & changing Danny & was damp & slightly foul smelling when she'd arrived home where there was no one not even a note from Cleo so the hospital smock & uniform pants would be cleaned & dried & no evidence left that she'd done what *any* mother would surely do but not before *she'd considered ignoring the mess* — she can't change that part & didn't that prove something about her? Every night as she goes down the hall to say goodnight the 30-second trip tells the same story & ends w/ the same question.

If he was 9 months old he'd be holding his toes in fat fists over his face & gurgling to a tinkling music box as though it's his fingers & toes producing the melody. But he's 9/yrs old w/ legs like crumpled then re-straightened pipecleaners & his feet cross each other — the top of 1 foot pressing into the arch of the other. 1 arm tucked across his middle as though it's a little boy who went to bed w/ a belly ache — the other arm bigger & stronger waving the hand high over his face as he closes his eyes w/ mouth stretched in a wide-open grin & he lets loose a parrot shriek before noticing Teri is in the doorway.

His next shriek is softer just like the high airy sing-song of a little boy doing nursery rhymes. He is able to roll over &

uses the big hand to grasp the bars of his crib & pulls himself into a kneeling position. The soft white fishnet grazes the top of his blond curls 1 hand still beating the air — either waving or seeking to beat an invisible tomtom. Such a cherry-lipped smile it's easy to not see the crooked brown-spotted teeth caused by flawed incomplete enamel not that way for lack of brushing b/c Teri does brush them every time she puts him to bed but he clamps his mouth shut & just sucks the toothpaste unless she squeezes his cheeks between his jaws & forces the mouth open so he screams & beats her arm w/ that same stronger hand & tears roll down his cheeks.

Teri unties the crib net & lowers the rail to take Danny under the armpits & swings him once around giggling before separating his tight scissor legs & putting 1 on either side of her hip which she juts far out to 1 side for him to ride. Then sitting in a chair w/ Danny on 1 knee she does his horseback riding song.

> *This is the way the farmer rides*
> *the farmer rides the farmer rides*
> *this is the way the farmer rides*
> *plod plod plod*

Then faster her leg hops up & down & his laughter gurgles in his throat.

> *This is the way the lady rides*
> *the lady rides the lady rides*
> *this is the way the lady rides*
> *trot trot trot*

Fastest now his head bobbing like a spring-necked statue in the back window of an old Buick & his chuckle so deep in his chest he sounds like a man.

This is the way the jockey rides
the jockey rides the jockey rides
this is the way the jockey rides
gallop gallop gallop

The other heads in the other beds are turned w/ bright eyes peering through bars of the cribs w/ soft high sighs of some kind of pleasure but not enough aptitude to be jealous or demand a turn. But Danny will still do his parrot shriek when he's put back into the crib w/ enough more intelligence than the others to always want more than he gets.

Four.

There's a big difference between fine motor skills and any kind of cognitive impulse to *want* to pick up a block and put it into a coffee can. *Can* you do it and *will* you do it — two different questions. The group is a thorough mixture of haves and have-nots as far as physical ability is concerned, but — just as Cleo suspected even before she read the programs in her kids' charts — even the slightest level of *comprehension* of the block-and-can game is definitely missing from the therapy room during the fine motor session. There's a possibility Danny may gather some kind of gratification in dropping a block into a can, but he finds just as much in throwing it across the room, so what's the big reward that'll encourage him to work at getting 40% or 50% or even 60% into the can? He'll be having a grand time in therapy no matter what he's not accomplishing. Making the whole thing even more of a circus, he's supposed to do all his fine motor therapy while the braces are on and locked with his body tied to a thing that keeps him standing at the work table instead of sitting. Naturally he hates that even more than the scooterboard, and will twist, wrench and scream if not constantly distracted.

Among the others, Eddie is seven years old and can sit up by himself. His abdomen is hugely swollen from air he's swallowed. He looks like a seven-year-old retarded pregnant boy. Cleo wonders if the air comes out of him at night when he sleeps, but she's never seen him asleep and she's never seen him un-filled. He swallows the air while he manufactures spit. He has long, thin graceful fingers, capable of holding a bubble of spit between thumb and index finger, but that's all he *wants* to hold. When Teri puts a wooden block into his hand, he instantly coats it with saliva of a whipped consistency then delicately holds it up at eye-level, turning it slowly back and forth, while his other hand continues to draw strings of drool from his mouth. He seems to be conducting some kind of symphony. Windy likes to go to symphony concerts, where they play with each other, trying to see through the dark music what the blue-hairs will do when they start to smell it.

Teri's doing a pretty decent job entertaining Danny — hopping on one foot, then bouncing like a bunny, then skipping across the room to retrieve the blocks he's chucking one by one — but as soon as he's not receiving direct stimulation, he squeezes his eyes shut and screeches. If anyone's kid acted like that in a restaurant, Cleo would want to slap him, braces or not. Windy would probably shout *Hey, smack your kid!* Once Windy had said, "C'mon, admit it, sweetie, you've slugged those morons when no one was looking."

"Unbelievably enough, I haven't," Cleo had answered, "yet," imagining the evil smile she hoped she was exhibiting, and yet feeling more than halfway like a total poser because for some reason she'd never once even had an impulse to hit a kid here.

Teri's still with Danny, and Cleo is cleaning crust from Glen's eyes with a damp washcloth, when Bishop does his doorway-giving-birth entrance. He even stops halfway born, only his upper body through the barely opened door, and starts observing them from there. Teri stops chasing blocks and hovers over Danny from behind, holding her coffee can — decorated with flowered contact paper — sliding it around on the table and following Danny's waving fist, tapping his wrist with her other hand to get him to drop the block. Sometimes Teri manages to get the can slid underneath the block when he drops it. Danny slaps the tabletop with his strong hand until Teri puts another block into his reach. He grabs the edge of the coffee can instead, tipping it to its side, batting it off the table, then he squeals, grinning. Eddie lifts an elongated saliva creation high over his head. Troy bangs his helmet against the tabletop. Glen arches his back against the rigid positioning chair, eyes rolling toward Danny who's trying to throw a block but Teri's got his arm and is guiding it toward the can, and he's giggling until he suddenly starts to cry.

Bishop approaches, both arms hugging that notebook to his chest. "How's it going?"

"As you can see," Cleo says, draping the washcloth over the back of Glen's positioning chair, "it's fucked."

Bishop cocks his head slightly. "I beg your pardon?"

Teri is removing Danny from his standing-up contraption, unlocking his braces and seating him in his wheelchair. She's given him the coffee can which he's holding up to his face and looking into like a tunnel, humming to create reverberations.

"Fucked," Cleo repeats slowly.

Can she really blame Teri for her surreptitious migration to the other end of the room? She's done it herself more than once, like when Windy did her give-me-a-goddamn-refund routine for a leather skirt she'd already worn to a party.

Cleo picks up a chart. "How's this, it's for Glen, fine motor goal is to drop a block into the coffee can eight times in ten tries."

"Sounds reasonable. You think it's too easy?"

"This is Glen, have you met him yet?" Cleo rests her hand on the white-blond hair of the 5 year old in the wooden positioning chair. If it weren't for the diaper restraint that comes from under his bottom, up between his legs then ties around his waist to the back of the chair — keeping him bent in a sitting posture — he'd stiffen and arch, straighten his body and slide out of his seat. His arms are extended in front of his torso, elbows locked, hands closed in awkward straight-fingered fists with thumbs protruding like tongues and wrists bent 90 degrees in opposite directions.

"Hello, Glen," Bishop coos in a high syrupy whipped-butter voice, the kind of voice that on a woman could be an instant puddle-maker, but from this doughboy with gray lips makes her want to puke.

Teri has fastened Danny's tray table to his wheelchair and has the busybox in front of him. Cartoon characters pop up when the phone dial is rotated or the sliding lever is moved or the light switch is flipped. He's seen it a zillion times. She's standing behind Danny, leaning over, their heads cheek-to-cheek, an obvious strategic move to put both their backs toward Bishop and Cleo. Cleo can hear the lids pop up rhythmically. Then Danny's hand has a fistful of Teri's hair and she's forcing his fingers open and the lids stop popping. Teri delicately sings *We're Off to See the Wizard* — which had been on the TV last night and Teri left the set on in Angela's room when they left, *just in case*, she'd said. Danny releases Teri's hair to clap with his strong hand patting the back of his weak one.

"I'll bet you love your new toys," Bishop continues purring to Glen. "There'll be more fun every day from now on." He straightens and looks at Cleo who doesn't straighten the scowl she can feel pulling at her upper lip and making her eyes squint.

Bishop says, "He looks like he *wants* to —"

"Bullshit — he doesn't have opposing thumbs, he can't even *open* his hands by himself. Who wrote this fucked program?"

"Please watch your language. If you have a question about the programs, you can ask the therapist when she comes in next week. Until then, please continue as instructed."

"It's a waste of time. Get her in here tomorrow."

"She's on a once-a-week schedule, she has other facilities to visit tomorrow. In the future, if we show progress and our reassessment warrants it, maybe we'll merit getting another day per week with the therapist. That should be additional incentive for you."

The metal chart folder claps shut in Cleo's hands then claps again when she smacks it back on top of the stack of other charts. "Incentive," she says, her voice a thin drone, a practiced monotone since Windy will completely ignore her when she shrieks. "I don't need *incentive* to do my job ten fucking times better than anyone else in this shithole."

"Your job is to carry out the therapy programs."

"My job ...." She sucks in a deeper breath. "My job is and has always been to maintain the health and comfort of their bodies."

"Quality of life is the ability to function."

"But it's frustrating them out of their goddamn minds just because some ass-brained therapist learned the phases of fine-motor development in her undergraduate classes *last year*." Cleo's voice breaks open right into his pink and gray face.

"I'm not going to fire you, Miss Parkins," he says, taking a step backwards, raising the clutched notebook a little higher, over his heart, "because I believe your fierce dedication will be valuable to us once you witness the programs starting to work. I think you'll be fighting as adamantly *for* the program as you are now against it. You'll be a leader I can hold up as an example to the other aides."

Air catches, neither coming in nor going out her open mouth, until she gasps, "Fuck that. What these kids need —"

"*I'll* decide what the patients need," his voice as thin as his lips, then, "spend some time with a resident other than Danny," Bishop croons past her toward Teri. He turns and slips back out the partially closed door, the rear of his pants sort of puckered and creased as though his ass cheeks are sucked together.

Teri comes up softly behind Cleo and puts a hand on each of her shoulders, which is not Teri's usual m.o., touching without invitation. "Another touché," she says, slightly hoarse and throaty, into Cleo's ear — a damn good imitation of Windy's voice, but how would Teri know that? — then immediately, Teri retreats out of the intimate zone.

"Damn straight. We'll see who has the big fucking revelation." She watches Teri re-straightening Danny's braces and tying him to his scooterboard. "Teri, you *do* know it's bullshit, don't you?"

Did Teri hear her? Cleo's watching Teri watching Danny swing the scooterboard in a half circle, his crossed-eyes on the rubber ball that Teri's rolling under one foot, then Teri taps it into his reach and says, "Most of it."

Is it another thoughtless Teri response while she thinks about whatever she thinks about while she's singing or chit-chatting to Danny? Even though they talk steadily at work — does Cleo even know what Teri *thinks*? She might, if she ever spent any time at *all* with Teri at home, but Cleo contrives to be allowed to spend every weekend, as much as possible, at Windy's, and on weekday mornings, before Teri goes out to her lawns and bushes, Cleo is sleeping until 11 or 12 in order to stay up late, all night if possible. Does Cleo really not know her comrade-in-arms after all? She feels struck dumb when she should be demanding *What the hell does* THAT *mean?* Is Teri getting sucked into the whole fucked therapy fantasyland? Windy would've asked straight out, if she cared. No, Windy would've just shrugged and said *Suit yourself* and gone about her own business. Cleo doesn't even know what her own business is anymore. Designing to get Windy to let her stay the night Saturday, the additional maneuvering to be allowed more hours on Sunday? The desperate hours of sleep between 3 a.m. and noon? The hour or so hiding herself in a crowd on the university campus she used to attend before quitting after one semester, watching Windy go from the library to the commons to see who she's walking with? Or the payoff, the *dates*, like a hallucinogenic drug, hours snapping past in a gurgle. And yet isn't it as if all *that* added together is half her life and the measly four hours *here* the other half? Despite lack of sleep or worry about when the next date will be or how many hours she'll be granted, she's always miraculously been buoyed with an intense drive between 4 and 8 p.m., an energy she can't explain. But now she sits stupidly staring at a bright, long drool stretching from Glen's mouth to the table. Troy dozes, huge helmeted head hanging over three blocks placed in front of him a half hour ago. Eddie now finger-painting a curved line in a pool of saliva, over and over, over and over, the same curve, mixing his spit with Glen's on the tabletop.

5.

The so-far faceless therapist's bracing schedule for Danny proposes 2 hours between breakfast & lunch then 2 more hours after his nap starting about 3 PM which means the AM shift should leave him w/ the braces locked. Yet Teri usually arrives at work to find Danny in the braces but w/ the knee joints unlocked wiggling around on the floor outlined in metal. These are tendons & muscles w/ 9 years of shrinkage & retraction to be undone so 4/hrs a day seems little to ask. But instead of sitting next to him & talking or hand wrestling w/ his good hand the AM cows just unlock the braces when Danny cries so Teri has to get in another hour of braces somehow. Her deal w/ Danny is another braced hour after dinner earns those jockey rides on her knee. Sometimes there are ways to squeeze out a few additional minutes here & there. Like today a ride on the waterbed while she makes waves & sings *Pirates of the Caribbean* after diapering & before dinner — during therapy hour — helps him get in an extra thirty minutes on top of whatever the AM cows probably didn't do.

A body already bobbing gently on the rippling water surface of the bed. Jon the boardboy about 40 pounds at 14/yrs old w/ hands in permanent fists & arms like burnt twigs crossed over a concave chest. Those arms can be moved just far enough away from the chest to thread a pajama top onto 1 arm flip it around the back then thread onto the other arm. Legs likewise brittle as deadwood w/ knees like a bulging burl in a branch & head constantly turned sharply to the left. His butt flat as a plank w/ an anus just a darkened knothole which every other day or so squeezes out a dollop of poop which flattens like a coin between his hard ass & stiff diaper.

"Jon" Teri says putting a foot on the water mattress & pushing up & down until Jon bounces like a flat-bottomed ship on choppy seas mouth opening & closing like a gasping fish. "One quick ride, Jonny, then Danny and I are gonna kick back here."

"He's having physical therapy" Cleo says from the rocker on the other side of the bed.

"On the waterbed?"

"Where else? At least he gets to feel something different. I can't *range* him, his joints don't move. And look at the bedsore, it's no better."

Cleo's voice is unusually dry & flat like a monotone comedian's distorted style of feigned boredom & can be both funny & frightening like when she uses it to mutter her disgust about 1 of the AM cows being a pig. But it should only be alarming to the *object* of her scorn & Teri isn't sure who that is at this moment since she's the only one in the room besides Jon & Danny.

Teri lifts the loose gauze on Jon's shoulder & sees the dry hole big as a half dollar w/ the bone showing in the middle like a white pupil in a red eye.

Danny's still unlocked so he's crawling like a determined man walking arm over arm toward his rubber ball in a far corner his usually noiseless glide over the easy linoleum floor of the therapy room sounding now of metal tapping & scraping.

"What're you planning to do with Danny — it's not his day for fine motor." Cleo rocks a little harder & something like sand grinds between the floor & the chair's runners.

"I'll do his range-of-motion then lock the braces and bounce him on the waterbed."

Cleo grunts & stands abruptly & the rocking chair hops backwards behind her then continues rocking by itself still grinding sand. She puts a cylinder-shaped bolster on the waterbed & tilts Jon so he's lying on 1 thin shoulder w/ his back propped against the bolster & the bedsore shoulder is up away from the mattress & his face is looking toward the ceiling. His lids blink & blink over big cowy eyes & his mouth opens & closes w/ thick lips dry like he's thirsty & Cleo gives him a sip of purple juice from a cup w/ a baby drinking nozzle on it but the purple comes running out his mouth & wets the sheet covering the waterbed.

Suddenly Cleo is talking again. "If you still have doubts, Teri — have you read Jon's chart?"

"Not really. I mean, no. Should I have?"

Crossing her arms & staring as though waiting for Teri to finish being such a namby-pamby then Cleo says "He's blind and deaf."

"Blind *and* deaf?"

"Yup. And wanna know what's in his chart for his therapy?" Cleo chants snidely — "*To be able to turn in the direction of a noise source.*"

Danny's ball rolls softly against Teri's ankle & she sends it another direction for him to follow. The braces click & scrape & click & scrape.

"Three times in five tries" Cleo finishes.

"Did you just find this out? Is this what you're mad about today?"

"If you don't *know* why I'm mad, just forget it."

Teri splashes onto the mattress next to Jon making him slip away from the bolster & slide a little more toward being on his back again instead of his side & the bedsore touches the vinyl bolster.

"Careful, I'm trying to get that thing to heal!" Cleo barks & Teri startles but is immobile w/ her butt too deep into the bouncy waterbed mattress & can't get up fast enough to help Cleo reposition Jon w/ the bolster.

"Sorry ... but keep it down, unless you want Bishop in here watching us again."

Cleo lies face down on the waterbed on the other side of Jon. Cleo's body alongside the bolster keeps it from sliding away from Jon & keeps him propped onto his side which is really like balancing a board on its edge instead of lying it flat — it has to have something to lean against or the 1st little breeze will knock it flat.

"God, maybe it's just PMS." Cleo's voice buried in the waterbed is fat & muffled almost like her head is actually underwater. "Except I already started and have *vicious* cramps."

"Is that unusual?" Teri carefully reclines backwards so now the 3 of them are parallel but w/ Teri on her back & Jon sort of tipped on his side & Cleo on her stomach.

"Always have 'em bad until the baby comes out."

"The *what*?" Teri bolts upright. Jon seems to blink more rapidly but maybe it's just that he blinks whatever rhythm is made by the waves in the waterbed — she's seen him do anything from slow to quicker to practically a flutter. Danny has the ball wedged between his weak arm & the wall & pounds it like a drum w/ his strong hand then grins a goofy grin over toward the bed & Teri calls "That's pretty funny Little Man!" b/c if he didn't get the validation he was obviously looking for he 1st of all wouldn't try out new behaviors & 2ndly would scream & then likely cry.

Cleo says w/o lifting her face from the waterbed "It's just a saying I have. The thickest hard part of the junk that comes out, the stuff like jelly, I call it the baby, after it's out the cramps go away. But I forgot you breeders are sensitive about stuff like that."

"*Breeders?*" Teri's pretty sure Cleo doesn't know about her little girl — *Sharon* was her name & still is unless she changed it to remove any trace of the mother who didn't ask to but bore & named her anyway. "Do you even *realize* how nasty and hostile —"

"Pardon my dust" Cleo says even more snotty then sits up & takes a nail clipper from her pocket. She liberates each of Jon's brittle fingers from his perpetual fist & makes 6 or 7 clips on each nail so his nails won't gouge into the flesh on his palm which is what would happen if they were never cut — just keep growing right into his skin. They know it has happened already at least once b/c when he was moved into Cleo's group they found dried blood under his nails & matching cuts in his palms.

"Sometimes it seems like you people think you can just say *any*thing." Teri lunges off the bed & goes to pick up Danny to remove his braces & change him so she can do his range-of-motion then get in at least 15 minutes w/ the braces locked.

"You *people*?" Cleo looks up glaring. "Now I'm *you people*?"

Naked Danny is a little tadpole w/ pinched bottom & tiny white hips & little flipper feet pointing toward each other. "We'll have to do some bodybuilding down here, the braces can't be the only things holding you up."

"So just ignore me, that's good, really mature."

"Maybe that's best until you're finished with your irrational attacks on —"

"Oh where'd you get *that*?"

"You call me a *breeder* then get all offended to be called *people*?" She stands w/ feet straddling Danny who's still on the floor naked the clean diaper under her arm the dirty 1 in her fist. He pats the back of her knee she flings the wet diaper against the wall. "You don't know *any*thing about me. For all you know I've had ten miscarriages, but you're hostile over being called *people*? Real compassionate, Cleo, shows how much —"

"Just shut up. God, your fucking *sensitivity* is making me *sick*."

The door makes a suction sound when it's opened quickly & sucks away any words Teri might've said. Bishop is standing there. Cleo gets up & wraps Jon in a sheet like a long thin papoose but one which doesn't bend when she picks him up & carries him in 2 arms out of the therapy room brushing past Bishop as though he weren't there. Teri finishes Danny's diaper & keeps her burning eyes on her fumbling fingers buckling the braces & tying the shoes & untangling Danny's fingers from her hair. When she's finished & Danny's legs are straight & his face is puckering about to cry she looks up & Bishop is gone the door still open less than halfway his usual entrance & exit.

Teri finishes tying Danny to the scooterboard so he takes off as soon as he's released as soon as she turns her back to retrieve the wet diaper & drops it on the pile of soiled linen Cleo had already stripped from the waterbed when she'd 1st come in. Then Teri is back on the waterbed & says "Come over here Danny" but she's staring at the ceiling not at him. Footsteps in the hall again & Teri rolls to her side & props her head up w/ 1 hand. It's Cleo coming back for the dirty linen & behind her Bishop again standing in the doorway w/ the notebook under 1 arm & 1 hand on the doorknob like a nun in Catholic school — an old trick coming into the bathroom to see if you're smoking & almost catching you the 1st time then coming back again in 5 minutes.

He looks at Teri on the waterbed. "Are you getting your oscillation stimulation?"

"You bet."

He turns sharply & leaves his crepe soles as squeaky as a nurse's as squeaky as her own. Cleo's making a tight bundle of the laundry as though she has to carry it half a mile instead of 10 feet down the hall. She didn't even need to come back for the laundry at all. Obviously stalling — what's her problem today or is it really just *OTR p.r.n.*? No it's got to be something else making Cleo purposely not look at Teri but not leave either.

Flexing & relaxing her thighs & butt over & over Teri makes waves on the bed that almost start to lift her body off the mattress w/ each thrust. "I should've told him to come here and give it to me himself."

Another shadow in the doorway. Teri bounds from the bed — heart jerking ears pounding but it's not Bishop it's a woman w/ red dutch-boy hair & a black scarf at her throat & a sleeveless white silk jumpsuit — the billowy legs tucked into ankle-high cowboy boots & cinched at the waist w/ a 2-inch wide black leather belt.

"Windy" Cleo says.

Six.

Is Cleo feeling this pissy just because Teri is apparently buying into Bishop's *dreams-do-come-true, it-can-happen-to-you* motto, or was it (more likely) because — until yesterday — she hadn't seen Windy for a week? Why should Cleo give a fuck what Teri thinks? If she was pissy before, she's got to be a veritable bitchwitch now. Practically shredding sheets as she whips old linen from mattresses, then bashing beds against walls after making airtight hospital corners with sheets so limp you can see through them, chucking dirty lunch dishes into a plastic tub — Glen thinks it's funny and arches his body, giggling with dimples, which makes Cleo slam up the crib rails after changing the adjacent empty bed then crash the crib back into place against the wall.

No dialogue coming from Teri's rooms across the hall, but Cleo can hear some inane prattle with Danny who doesn't mind if you say the same thing to him fifty times in a row. He's learned to make a sucking sound with his tongue — his version of kissing — so when you say *Gimme-a-kiss* he responds willingly with a spitty raspberry, and unlike a trained dog, you don't have to give him a cookie. Just being allowed to *do* his schtick is reward enough. That counts for almost anything he can do except his fine motor tasks, which, of course, according to the almighty program, means learning to kiss counts for nothing. He's lying on his back in the hall with his scooterboard tied to his stomach and every five minutes Teri asks him for another kiss. There's a lot of sloshing and flushing in Teri's bathroom, the sound of wet diapers splatting on the floor, which probably means Teri isn't going to the laundry chute with each piece of laundry, instead saving it for one big trip later, avoiding coming out in the hall where Cleo might happen to be passing by.

But Cleo's so pissy *she's* not going into the hall either, even though it's occurred to her that by the time she needs to put Angela to bed, she'll either have to ask Teri to help or make the rift *real* obvious by going down to the nurse's station to ask someone else.

Was Teri just giving Cleo space because she feels weird about Windy? Then it's twice as weird for Cleo, having brought Windy to climax in a great many places, but, until yesterday, not in the hospital. Teri hadn't ever seen Windy before, so on top of an unexpected first meeting, there's the possibility Teri knows what happened in the therapy room after she left. And it really wasn't the existing tension with Teri that had prevented Cleo from going out into the hall, after Windy was gone, to say *That was my girlfriend and now she wants to have an open relationship*. No, the reason she couldn't tell Teri was that not only *after* Windy's big news but *during* being informed that

Windy was fucking someone else, Cleo went ahead and made it with Windy herself, desperately, as though if she were good enough, if Windy's orgasm were wild enough, it would keep her from pursuing her on-the-side titillation of *fucking a man's wife better than the prick-owner himself could do it*, as Windy had unabashedly put it.

Teri had scooted out of the therapy room before any introductions could be made. But she hadn't left before Windy had said, "Well, girls, I managed to get this far without seeing any monsters, but before I come any farther, I gotta know if the coast is clear in here." Normally Cleo would've instantly shared a glance of disgust with Teri, but in that nearly blinding white-hot second she knew she wouldn't, *couldn't* because she (a) had to be loyal to Windy and (b) wasn't even sure she *was* allied with Teri anymore. But as soon as Windy spoke, Teri beat it out of there, even ducking right under Windy's pale-as-white-silk arm, holding the door open. Windy's jumpsuit was unbuttoned to down between her tits, casually not really exposing anything, a sign Cleo could read anywhere, but *here?* Windy *hated* the hospital.

"Alone at last. Can I close the door?" Windy had asked, closing it.

"Well, people could come in any time."

"All the better. Danger is life's cilantro."

"Well, one danger is that I won't get my work done in time."

"So you turn into a pumpkin at the strike of eight? Get rid of those stinking rags."

Cleo had instantly tossed the armload aside, and Windy was striding forward, silk whispering between her thighs, pulling Cleo close and sinking her teeth tenderly into Cleo's neck, and, right on cue, the ripple of chills started in her gut.

"Lose the smock, okay? It stinks like piss."

Cleo's fingers were immediately, obediently undoing her buttons and didn't stop, even when Windy, sitting on the edge of the rocker with legs crossed — the sharp toe of one boot bouncing — said, "I've been perusing the personals, just for the hell of it, you know? And guess what I found? This house-wife who's hot for chicks but doesn't want to admit it. She likes me to strap on a dildo and fuck her like a dog."

By that time Cleo was naked from the waist up, standing in front of Windy, then straddling her legs and sitting on her lap while Windy pinched a nipple between each thumb and forefinger. Where was her self respect, her outrage? Hadn't she heard what the fucking bitch had just *said*?

"I'll do that with you, Windy," Cleo had rasped, her chin hooked over the top of Windy's head. "I mean ... if that's what you want, you don't need anyone else."

"I wish I could share her with you, but she's not into trios ... *yet!*" Windy looked up and kissed Cleo's mouth.

When Windy's tongue was out of Cleo's mouth and back to making tight circles around her tits, Cleo said, in a weird childlike whine she'd barely recognized as her own voice, "No, I mean ... I thought we had a ... you know, committed thing going."

"I think an open relationship is what I want right now. You can do the same with your live-in. You can't tell me you two haven't been doing it."

Cleo backed up onto her feet again as Windy rose out of the rocking chair. "Teri and I are just friends, it would ruin our ... alliance. If it even exists anymore."

"Fine, I don't care, do whatever." Windy slithered onto the waterbed, looked up past her half-lowered shaded eyelids

— she'd obviously been to the salon for her make-up today — patted the mattress beside her.

"Teri's been weird lately," Cleo had said, lying down and cuddling close to Windy, her back against Windy's front. "Like just before you came in, Teri said she'd like to get our barfbag boss to give her oscillation stimulation — I mean, she was joking, it's a therapy we're supposed to do on the waterbed. But lately she *never* makes jokes like that. I think she actually *believes* this pathetic therapy is going to do some good. It's really come between us."

"Just make your six bucks an hour and forget the shithouse exists the rest of the day. You've got better things to do." And Windy was turning Cleo around, taking Cleo's hand and showing her fingers the way between the jumpsuit's pearl buttons.

The dinner carts had already arrived by the time Cleo sneaked Windy downstairs to the laundry room and out the basement door. She apologized to Angela and Glen and the other kids who had to eat their dinners in wet diapers. They'd all been changed during her first half-hour at work, but, partly because of going ballistic with Teri, she hadn't had time to check them all again before Windy showed up, and she'd neglected them to go ballistic with Windy too, so to speak.

Danny's been shrieking a shrill repetitive note for several minutes, and Cleo realizes she not only can't hear Teri at all anymore, but Teri's TVs are turned down too. That's unusual. Cleo doesn't usually have her TVs on loud enough to hear unless you're right in front, where the kids are, and even then you'd have to really be concentrating. But Teri's sets are usually always practically blaring. Cleo pokes just her head around the doorway. Teri is standing outside one of her own doors, across the hall, very still, one leg and one shoulder leaning on the wall beside the open doorway, cheek pressed against the doorjamb, her little stub ponytail hanging limply as though beaten and tired. Her other shoulder and leg and half her head make half a silhouette in the doorway, because the drapes covering the bright western window inside the room are obviously pulled aside.

"What is it?" Cleo asks softly, moving up behind Teri.

But Teri doesn't need to answer — and she doesn't. It's Jon's mother. She's taken him out of his own room and found the rocking chair that Teri keeps stealing to put beside Danny's bed by the sunny window. The mother has Jon dressed in new dotted pajamas and tucked inside a soft yellow baby blanket. His feet sticking out the end are burnt sticks. The woman rocks him, humming, cradling him in her arms, his flat bottom balanced on her leg, his shoulder leaning up against her arm. Like holding a plank, like hugging a board.

His eyeballs are marbles that roll back and forth. His head as usual turns sharply to his right, this time toward his mother. He moans, his thick lips pulling away from yellow teeth. And under his blanket his twig arms are crossed, Cleo knows, like a corpse. Yellow sun is coming through the window, creating a brilliant block of flying dust, making the whole scene a little fuzzier, washed out, over-exposed.

Someone moves beside Cleo, on her other side, and it's not Teri — it's Sister Bishop. He hugs his organizational notebook with both arms to his heart, and while he looks at Jon, at Jon's mother, Cleo can see muscles tighten, relax, tighten, relax on his pinkish grey jawbone below his ear.

The ward suddenly seems quiet when Jon stops moaning. Even Danny is quiet, there's just the drone of Jon's mother's closed-mouthed hum, the soft wood-against-linoleum grind of the rocker, and then Bishop's overly moist breath on her neck making her want to barf. He's whispering, "It's his birthday. Today. He's 15."

As though *he* knows anything about Jon, as though this strange woman who probably decided just today to call herself his mother knows anything. After all, *Cleo's* the one who pushes Jon's thick tongue down with the spoon, trying to get most of the pureed spinach or some kind of meat to go down his throat; *she's* the one who cleans his face when his eyes get crusty or he drools a puddle under his cheek; *she's* the one who washes his half-dollar-sized armpits which can sweat like any 14 — excuse me, 15-year-old — boy's. In fact Cleo's the one who bathes his entire body and knows every crease of it, including the almost-regular sized uncircumcised penis, and the anus which resembles a smashed raisin — as does his shit, sometimes. Who is this fake Bozo standing here like a gushing, tear-jerking talk show host pretending to worry about someone he's only actually *seen* once and, if he chooses, never has to see *again*?

"Well," Cleo says, not in a whisper, more like the TV when people are talking, even shouting, but the volume's turned very low, "Happy birthday. I guess that means he's had that bedsore for one fifteenth of his life."

Bishop turns slowly, like a head pivoting on a mechanical mannequin, and she feels him stare with his opaque blue eyes at the side of her face as though she's standing there gossiping with Teri, as usual, like any other afternoon at work, without realizing he's listening. But Teri acts like she hears nothing, and says nothing.

"Yeah," Cleo goes ahead by herself with what should've been a two-way exchange, "and I got him up to fifty pounds yesterday ... congratulations ... thank you very much, but so far his therapy program has been a problem for me ... oh yeah, Cleo? How so ... well — and I won't bother to mention how him being both blind and deaf affects the occupational therapy goal — but giving him range-of-motion is like trying to bend a carrot. Ever try to bend a carrot? It probably doesn't *feel* good if you're a carrot and someone's trying to bend you!" Then Cleo laughs, still not loud, but, she hopes, crudely.

Bishop's voice is like a toy, coming out of a doll or animated stuffed bear, "These are the people we're really working for. For parents like this one, for kids to know they have a place, for both to belong to each other."

Cleo's pointing down her throat with one finger, but Teri actually *sighs*!

"Too bad we need more money to keep doing it," he pipes before floating into the sunlit room, opening the notebook to show Jon's mother the therapy program, his therapist's assessment, and a copy of a colorful chart — a positioning graph for Jon, a turning schedule, to keep him off that shoulder. "That way," he tells the mother, "it will heal in no time at all. And," he adds, "I want you to know, we're very close to being able to continue to fund all of Jon's programs for another year."

She tries to say *God what a phony* out loud, but there's no one to say it to and no one to listen. Teri is no longer in the doorway. Behind Cleo, Danny's scooterboard is rumbling down the carpeted hall and clattering into the therapy room, Danny laughing like an excited girl, Teri bent over and running behind him, her hands on his butt, pushing him.

7.

Her stomach & ankles itch b/c there's sometimes too little time to change after mowing lawns. Today Teri just peeled the t-shirt off then applied more deodorant & zipped up a smock from yesterday but didn't change the jeans or shoes & there're grass clippings in her socks & in her waistband & stuck to the skin on her neck w/ dried sweat. She probably smells like the dumpster in the alley where she empties the mower bag — fresh green pungent scent of healthy turf mixed w/ rotting garbage of every sort. But Bishop & Cleo both probably have noses like hers too cauterized to smell anything anymore & how would Danny know an acceptable scent from a vulgar one so who cares when there's no one to offend. But she leaves him alone in the therapy room for a second anyway & goes to 1 of her rooms — the other 1 not the 1 where Jon's mother still has him on her lap in the rocking chair — & gets the baby powder from Cheryl's dresser. She shoots a geyser of smoky powder up under each armpit & sprinkles some into her collar both down her back & onto her breasts. Then bats the air to clear the haze of swirling talc. Cheryl smiles & coughs w/ her hands joined together above her tray table like a child about to do a recitation in class & she coughs again & sneezes. The toddler Sharon's eyes would run & throat would hack when Teri wore perfume & she would cover her whole face w/ 2 tiny hands & run to bury eyes & nose in the 1st roommate's lap & never seemed to notice how rancid *he* could get. A decent idea in theory to advertise for a roommate — w/ stipulation *handicapped preferred* for several good reasons — offering free rent in exchange for child care. So a wheelchair-bound MS patient traded baby-sitting for 24/hr in-house home care meaning he was there w/o leaving for 2 or 3 years & his condition getting worse. Every shower meant Teri had to wipe down the ceiling & walls & floor w/ every towel in the house so by unspoken mutual agreement his bathing tapered off to once a week then every other week then once a month. The little house had been built for a WWII military couple not a handi-capable — the PC lingo for disabled he'd insisted she use when referring to his condition — so wheelchair access was limited to rolling in between sink & toilet until his feet hit the tub then rolling backwards back out which meant he had to use a removable shower massage & just let the whole bathroom be his shower stall & there was still rotting wood under the floor.

Returning to the therapy room she finds Danny surrounded by big wooden beads meant for stringing together on a fat yarn rope which is an advanced fine motor skill. From his prone position on the scooterboard he has reached the red plastic crate on the 2nd shelf pulled it out & tipped it over so the colored wooden beads half as big as baseballs roll around him much quicker than his delighted crossed-eyes can follow. Both his hands — strong & weak — are held up & out as though waiting to catch a butterfly when it alights on a flower.

While on the floor on hands & knees collecting the over-large unstrung beads Teri keeps Danny listening & watching. "OK, Little Man, these are for when you're older, maybe next year, you pay attention and make sure I pick 'em all up, then we'll get you out of the braces for range-of-motion. It'll feel good to stretch, don'cha think?"

He says his newest word *buh!* while bouncing the strong hand in the air w/ fingers spread & flat palm down — a perfect pantomime of dribbling a basketball. It's his 3rd or 4th word w/ the others including *I-der* for Hi There & *muh-muh* for Mama which she realizes he says to everyone not just 1 person exclusively but since Teri's w/ him all afternoon 5 days a week she never actually hears him say it to anyone else.

Out of his braces & onto his back on the thick vinyl-covered foam mats she gives him a floppy-eared bunny as usual w/o eyes to hold & wave in the air while she gently grasps 1 leg at knee & ankle & slowly bends the knee until his heel touches his buttock then she uses his hip joint to move his knee toward his chest keeping foot flexed & toes up before slowly returning the leg to its usual halfway straight extension. *5 repetitions b.i.d. w/ each leg* the chart says. But Teri always does at least 10 w/ each leg b/c she can't assume the AM cow did any at all.

Early on she'd taken her little girl to her yard jobs — as a baby riding in a pack on Teri's back & when a toddler Teri *would've* given Sharon a toy mower & let her follow Teri's footsteps in the fresh cut path in the wake of the big machine — but the man whose sperm it was said he didn't want *his* baby girl losing a finger or toe & out in that sun looking like a granny by the time she was 2. Teri looks up once into the mirror behind Danny's head while she gives him range-of-motion but just sees the same sun-toughened face as always. Once Teri had thought she'd be a nurse but knows she loves to close her eyes with her face in the best honest sunshine of early spring and couldn't spend as much time indoors as students do & now it's too late. Sharon is what now — 12? 13? Is 31 old enough to be *old*? Old enough to have failed as a mother before the girl was even 8? The sperm-producer had been in the picture both before & after the declining MS patient's eventual demise — the roommate less & less able to care for a more & more mobile toddler until 1 day Teri found the handi-capable nanny on the floor able only to blink his eyes & Sharon in only underpants w/ her doll in a bedpan on the floor beside a puddle of the nanny's drool said *he peed his pants*. Hearing about it in who-knows-what kind of 4-yr-old's embellished detail the egg-fertilizer immediately began steadily to increase his time w/ the busily growing girl. His 1 weekend a month became 2 then all 4 then he switched to weekdays making the transition complete by the time the girl was 5 or 6 so Teri hardly remembers having Sharon at home much at all during the rapid-learning-of-things phases. Teri would return from mowing trimming edging & pruning to find the girl had learned colors & how to count using cars in daddy's showroom & gumballs from the machine in the sucker-born-every-minute waiting room. Then the trip to visit his mother in Texas & neither returned — the showroom after all just a place the sperm-man worked not something he owned. & wasn't it somehow a relief when it was over — a relief that the girl eventually no longer came home w/ stories of daddy's cars & daddy's computer? How can Teri admit *that*? — well she doesn't out loud.

Is Jon's mother still here? Teri wants to use the rocker for a few minutes of repose before the dinner carts arrive. Danny whaps her in the face w/ the bunny & says "buh!"

"Not a ball, a bunny. A blind bunny. *Isn't that funny / to be a blind bunny?*"

"Buh!"

It's Cleo who picks the glass eyes out of the stuffed animals every time a different one shows up — castoffs donated by the hospital recreation volunteers who run bingo games for the geriatrics or childhood teddies bought by aides for their favorites or new bunnies or dogs or birds or even dinosaurs brought by parents on birthdays. Invariably vomited on spit on peed on then recycled through the wash they end up in someone else's room or the patient is transferred but the toys stay behind. Teri caught Cleo 1 day w/ an armload of blind puppies & bears returning them to the baby room. "The eyes're dangerous" she'd said simply. "They might bite one off and swallow it." Even though most of them can barely swallow their pureed diets.

"Ah ha, getting our therapy are we?" It's a man practically a boy in khaki pants & golf shirt w/ a stack of charts in his arm. The door slowly creaks back to a halfway open position. "Let's see, this is …" He clicks through the charts like huge metal playing cards. "Daniel Murphy, right? And you're …?"

"Teri Lightner." She answers before asking who the hell he is but he's already making notes in a chart w/ a black pen not green so he's no nurse nor aide & what's left for him to be since he's too young to be an administrator & they never come down here anyway & there's only 1 of Bishop — so he's got to be the physical therapist who she's never seen b/c he usually comes during the cow shift.

"I heard you were here!" Cleo bangs the door against the wall w/ 1 foot b/c she's carrying Jon back into the therapy room but still wrapped in his new birthday blanket. "I want you to look at this one." Not talking to Teri in fact walking right past so she can put Jon onto the waterbed then turns & looks over Teri's head at the boy-therapist. Teri continues Danny's range-of-motion but she's lost count of her repetitions & Danny's getting squirmy trying to twist onto his stomach to watch the young man who has already put his stack of charts on the upper shelf & is obediently walking around Danny to go stand beside Cleo & they're both just standing there looking down at Jon. Teri sings in rhythm w/ Danny's exercises *Yo ho yo ho a pirate's life for me.*

"Well?" the boy-therapist says.

"Is that all you can say? What the hell kind of program is this you've got for him?" Cleo swings a chart at the therapist which if it were an ax & kept going would've cut him in half at the waist but the flat metal chart stops & he claps both hands on top & bottom catching it as Cleo lets go.

"Yes, I recommended range-of-motion —"

"It's impossible."

"OK, if he's too rigid you certainly shouldn't force the joints. It's a standard program to prevent further rigidity."

"*Further* rigidity. I think he's hit the end of the road as far as rigidity goes."

"We can usually bring back some range, even if barely discernible."

"Go ahead, try it on him. I'll bet you haven't even touched him yourself." Cleo crosses her arms.

"I must've, before I wrote the program." But still obediently he kneels & cups Jon's elbow while his other hand makes an attempt to move Jon's forearm out of the immutable right angle. "Yes, he's pretty bad, I agree."

"Okay, what about the rest of this idiotic therapy?"

"That's the occupational therapist's program."

"Oh, she wants him to have an *occupation*!" Cleo shrieks her wicked-witch laugh the one they'd both been using as a joke after *The Wizard of Oz* was on TV a while back.

The therapist wheels & returns to stand over Danny who's about at the end of his road as far as lying in 1 place is concerned. He's chucked the rabbit out of reach & his upper body is twisted around as though attempting to go crawl after the toy w/o bringing his legs w/ him.

"Well, your program looks like it's going fine" the therapist says reaching over Danny to slide his chart from the top of the stack on the shelf. "We'll get those hamstrings straightened out."

"Muh-muh." Danny lets his shoulders return to the mat & grins up at the man while holding his weak hand w/ his strong 1 then starting to patty-cake strong palm slapping weak knuckles.

"Yes, mama will be proud of you." This boy-therapist must've worked his way through college w/ baby-sitting — perfectly natural talking w/ kids in a way maybe Teri never was before the wing changed from geriatric to moron. Too late for her own but Sharon's too old now anyway to be talked to like this.

He picks up the empty braces. "But if you keep growing, muh-muh will need to buy a new set of braces, looks like these've been adjusted as far as they'll go."

"So, the next ones —" Teri says & takes the braces from him so she can put them back on Danny. "Will they have better joints — looser ones? He can move the knee joints by himself but I don't think he can move the hips. And will the shoe be built up on the bottom so his feet are level?"

"I'm glad to see you girls are so on top of your patients' programs." The young therapist smiles at Teri still putting the braces on Danny then at Cleo who's got her back to Jon w/ arms still folded & brows lowered just staring & scowling like there's something disgusting happening in front of her face. But she's seen Teri tie Danny to his scooterboard 1000 times before. "But Daniel doesn't need to be moving the joints of the braces himself. He won't be getting braces for walking."

The towel rips somewhere as Teri tightens the knot around Danny. She releases him & stands upright not realizing she's only a foot or so from the boy therapist's face. A lineless pleasant face w/ intelligent enough eyes but w/o much more expression than that — not joy nor sorrow nor anything in-between. Just pleasantness. Like it's pleasant to be here in this sunny room w/ so many toys & big red vinyl bolsters of several shapes & a waterbed w/ bright flowered bedspread & padded floor mats & a little boy chasing a stuffed blind bunny.

"Why?" The soft word flashes into the pleasant sunny room like heat lightning.

"Daniel won't walk." The therapist's voice is still balmy. "He hasn't the mental capacity to learn it. He'll never have the physical capability."

"Then —"

Interrupted by Cleo's snort.

Then *what*? No Teri had nothing more to say anyway. Instinctively before she can stop herself shoots a glance at Cleo but quickly switches to something that feels like a wince but she hopes it's a wry wise smile on 1 side of her mouth at the therapist who's not looking at her anymore anyway. Doesn't return Danny's idiotic grimace. He pats her calf & says "*I-der*!" then *so* expertly swings his chrome chassis & 4 wheels into a new direction & heads off as though he has somewhere to go & something important to do.

Eight.

By giving herself all of the eight-minute leeway on either side of the official 8 p.m. shift-change — clocking out at 7:53 — Cleo can get to Windy's radio station by 8:15, right in the middle of the ten-minute window when Windy might be leaving. She's done it for dates dozens of times, impelled to slash shamelessly through traffic by a so-far unverified fear that Windy won't bother to wait if Cleo gets there after 8:20. But tonight there'd been no date, not a scheduled one, she hadn't managed to get Windy to commit to going out when she'd visited the hospital — just yesterday! So it's another evening in her room, door closed, pretending the room isn't attached to a house with Teri in it, padding softly from living room to kitchen, TV barely murmuring, tentative clink of dishes, someone obviously trying to make no noise, a prowler in her own house — now she's a soft hushy voice on her telephone with the TV humming along like white noise.

Cleo's got a radio — she could hammer through the taut calm with a sports broadcast or find a rap station. But she might as well not move, stay here completely flaccidly motionless and curled in kidney-bean shape on a narrow child's bed with purple faded, frayed bedspread, might as well wallow in her apparent shallowness — not deep enough for anyone to ever drown there! Isn't that exactly what Windy would say if she saw Cleo now, if she happened by the window with her dildo-fetishist *companion* who, it turned out, was not a bored housewife but a newswriter married to a pony-tailed suit at the station, and *she'd* had a date with Windy tonight, but Cleo managed to get Windy to sit with her in her idling car for fifteen minutes until Windy *had* to go or she'd be late meeting *Trish* at the Howard Johnson near the beach.

The scene-change music on the TV croons dolefully, then shimmers, fades, a voice in an empty, hollow room. Or is that Teri? Perhaps Teri's discussing what Cleo overheard earlier at the hospital: the offer Teri had once again received, a opportunity to move to the full time a.m. shift. But no. Teri speaks only one or two words at a time, then long stretches of quiet listening. And not for a while now. Maybe the call has ended. Teri would've put the phone down gingerly, no *tink* of protest from a receiver dropped rudely into the cradle, like often after one of Cleo's calls, like Cleo *certainly* would've done if she'd spoken to Windy on the phone tonight, instead of in the car. The phone wouldn't've even been in one piece anymore.

9.

Teri can't help thinking Sharon's 12 or is it 13-yr-old voice is sweet & feminine like Bishop's & it's probably another sign of how bad she is at being a mother to still be thinking of trivialities of the hospital & the 4 hours out of 24 spent there instead of being moved & touched by the gentle winsome sound of Sharon's voice answering the phone & at long last being able to hold the receiver tight & speak w/ her.

But — "I'm not Sharon, I'm *Shannon*" is what the angelic voice says perhaps before realizing it's her mother or at least Teri wants to be her mother & that's probably what she should've said instead of "Hi Sharon, it's me."

"What can I do?" Teri says. "I'd like it so much if you would visit me."

"I, I, I, me, me, me —" the child responds. "You never change."

"Tell me what to change." It's a whisper & perhaps the

girl didn't hear. "I can be a better mother. I've been practicing. With a little boy."

"Why would you do that? You *hate* boys."

"I do?"

"Yeah. Dad says so."

"But Sharon, I — "

"*Shannon.* I shouldn't be talking to you. You'll poison me."

"Does he say that too?"

"I know all about it now!" the girl exclaims & there's no giggle or lisp or anything silly girlish just the clear bloom of her pure honest voice. "I know you didn't want me because Daddy was a boy and you hate boys. He said he was making love — "

"He said *making love* to you? He told you about … intercourse?"

"I know a lot of things, like how you were some kind of weirdo zombie, he said, like making love to a crash-test dummy, he said, and maybe you were drunk or stoned and, like, didn't even know it was *happening* so it made him afraid, he said, especially, like, when he called and called for weeks afterwards, but you never called him *back*."

"But, honey, I was —"

Wait — no — he'd never called there'd been no message how could there be she hadn't had an answering machine no need for 1 she barely dated. "What is he telling you?" A murmur perhaps not meant for the girl to hear.

"The *truth*" proclaims the ingenuous voice of her erstwhile child not speaking as a child — *what* had she been told? "He told me how when you finally told him you were pregnant, you said it like you'd been shot." Must be exactly what he said this story coming out too well-worded & phrased but — is *this* what happened? "And he tried to do the right thing, like, he would've married you, at least for a while, but *you* said no. *You* rejected *him*." Yes she surely would've if that's what he'd said but she'd never *told* him she'd conceived he'd found out some other way that she can't remember now. After the briefest of pauses perhaps hopeful for an answer but not willing to wait very long she can hear the girl breathe in then the voice is once again feathery for a moment & almost sounds like she did at 6 or 7 before speeding up & crystallizing — "I used to ask why you didn't come with me to visit Daddy and you always said he didn't want you. What a lie. He *offered*. He told me what you said back, that you wanted an abortion instead of having me!" No hint of tearful wobble in the fresh & furious intonation.

"Honey, every pregnant unmarried girl at least *thinks* about maybe doing that, even if she's thinking, *no I won't do that*. Don't you understand?"

"No! Daddy says the only reason you didn't is you're just too lazy and put it off and waited too long until it was too late, or expected him to pay you to do it which you know he'd never do in a million years."

Why doesn't she remember this? Why can she only remember dealing w/ the unrequested sperm donor *after* the girl was already born a robust baby then an agile & curious toddler then a clever lively little girl running everywhere on filly legs. An *unplanned* pregnancy they call it now not *illegitimate*. Hadn't it been more like immaculate conception — not asked for but then not damned nor denounced & she never thought to tell or blame the Y chromosome he just took the credit then eventually took the girl as though she'd pushed herself out from between *his* legs.

"Honey, I — I'm sorry you had to hear all this, but it's .... Your father might have misunderstood me."

"No way, you were always against him, I remember, if you couldn't keep him from seeing me, you wanted me to hate him. I also know the only reason you didn't let someone else adopt me was because you knew *he* wanted me, you only kept me to keep *him* from adopting me."

"Sharon—"

"My name is *Shannon*, I don't want the name *you* chose."

"Oh, honey ... I ... I don't know why he's saying these things."

"Because he wants me to know what kind of person you are and what kind of person you were trying to turn me into. You would want me to be a manhater. He says you paralyzed him with your hate. But he recovered, he walks and runs and plays golf, he's a coach for my softball team, everyone's amazed how he used to be in a wheelchair."

"A wheelchair? You're confusing him with someone else."

"Maybe *you* are. He's my *father*. *You* accused him of rape and they questioned him and he had to quit school."

"What? No, I never said that word." Well now they *do* call it the date-rape drug but it had no name then xcept maybe like *he slipped her a Mickey* which is much too old-fashioned. But if she never even remembered the grind & thrust of copulation how could she say *rape*? She woke the next morning a little sore like from horseback riding & dirty like a yeast infection & in a week the nausea started *b.i.d.* Never even looked for the source of the single wiggling cell that had fertilized her egg somehow he found her & told the judge out loud in court *she was a virgin when we had sex* how did he know?

"Well I need to go, Daddy doesn't want me talking to you."

"You weren't old enough for me to explain to you what had happened. I will now if you want me to."

"I don't want anything more from you." Then the *tick* of disconnection.

Ten.

Another meeting, everyone sitting around the therapy room on the mats, on the waterbed, propped up with positioning bolsters, Bishop in the rocking chair that has once again been stolen from Teri's room, but whether or not Teri is annoyed or maybe brought the chair here for Bishop herself and held it for him while he softly lowered his pinched butt into the seat, Cleo doesn't know and can't bother herself with wondering. It's high time she concentrated on her own problems rather than expending valuable energy on her conquered, lilylivered roommate or this stinking place and the lame idiot running it.

Danny's on his scooterboard just inside the doorway, squealing and chirping. Bishop looks up from his notebook but doesn't start talking, a transparent pause calling for quiet, but Teri's staring at the bottom of one tennis shoe because she's sitting cross-legged and that's what's in front of her to stare at, so Cleo gets up, pushes Danny and his scooter out the door.

"Go play," she says, then shuts him out. When she turns back around, Teri is looking up, staring with some kind of sad glare. Cleo doesn't bother returning any particular expression, although she feels like sneering. She sits on the waterbed, then reclines and blinks up toward the blue ceiling.

After a moment, Bishop says, "The assessors are coming. As you know, they're going to decide whether or not we get fully re-funded for another two years. We may even get *more* money if they like what they see." A hesitation for emphasis, probably pursing his flaccid lips, tapping with the powder soft pads of his callusless fingers. "But the programs aren't happening the way they should."

Like they *should* ... everything's going *exactly* the way it should, blind kids can't see the colored blocks, spastic kids can't hold the wooden beads, deaf kids can't hear a wind-up music box. Is her whole life going to be one long exercise in submission to futility? You consent to your part of the bargain then the other person won't agree to jack shit. In the fifteen minutes Windy had bequeathed to Cleo last night in the car outside the radio station, Cleo had agreed to the open relationship. Actually first Windy had said, "Hey if you can't cope, you can just blow me off, no skin off my nose." So Cleo said she could probably deal with the sexual freedom but at least hoped for something like emotional commitment or security, like could Windy just say she'd always be there for Cleo, that at least on *some* level they were partners? Then maybe in the future their partnership could deepen.

"Don't think so, girl," Windy calmly answered. "You know me. I'm frank about what I want. Maybe it's time for you to be a little more honest too."

"I just admitted to wanting a relationship with you."

"I think you admitted *needing* a relationship with me. That's pretty unattractive. And if I ever did get *that* down and serious about someone, there'd have to be some intellectual *edge*, know what I mean?"

"You're saying I'm just a Barbie doll?"

"This's what I'm talking about, babe, all those simple-minded clichés. Look, I might've lied yesterday. Trish isn't a housewife, she's a newswriter and works here, married to one of the suits." Windy had reached up and turned on the over-head light so she could examine the design painted on her thumbnail. "I admit the thing with her has an element of risk — that's what adds the garlic and tamales — if the suit finds out my butt'll be iced. And *she's* taking a chance too. She wants to get into television, and he could either help it happen or blackball her completely. That she'd jeopardize herself, that's a kick for me." Windy reached again to extinguish the light then took a single cigarette from the breast pocket of her purple silk vest-shirt. "But she's still keen on her career — her ambition sharpens her. And you know *I* plan to move up to videojock. But you ... you don't care or even *think* enough about any-thing, except your shithouse idiots and wanting to call me your girlfriend." The last part uttered with the cigarette between her lips. It bobbed up and down, marking the rhythm of the words. Then Windy had clicked her lighter, a flame appeared without the flare and sizzle of a match, the cigarette caught, glowed, and Windy's first exhalation of smoke streamed toward the windshield.

Someone moves, and the waterbed jiggles like a laughing stomach. A soft repeated thud at the door is the heel of Danny's palm.

"I am the program *director*," Bishop practically whines,

"but I can't make the programs *work*. We're a team. Without you girls, my job means nothing."

He finally understands his worth. The type of comment she might mutter to Teri, or write on her palm and flash sideways like crib notes. Cleo sits up. Teri is sitting on the floor mat, legs stretched out straight in front of herself, crossed ankle over ankle, her body propped up by her hands behind her butt. She's looking at Bishop with opaque eyes. Listening and concurring? Or just pretending to hear him while she's off somewhere else? Cleo thinks Teri may've cried some after her long phone conversation last night. It was difficult to tell when the conversation ended and whether Teri was crying *on* the phone or by herself. Or if she were maybe sighing. Or even singing. Eventually Cleo *had* recognized the trotting horse song Teri sings to Danny, but without words, just the tune, hummed like a dirge.

"Now I know everything isn't always a smooth road." Bishop effortlessly plucked *that* cliché from thin air. "And we don't always see quick results. I remember undergoing therapy myself, so I know ...."

Therapy for what? Being a milksop pantywaist? Now who's using clichés? Windy could come up with some fitting zingers for him. Cleo happens to be looking at Teri when Teri's chin drops as though whatever thin wire has been holding her head up has suddenly snapped. The opposite motion Cleo's head made last night when Windy said *see-ya* and got out of the car. Cleo's head had tipped slowly backwards until it hit the headrest, and the trite tears or her shallow neediness leaked across her temples into her hair.

"We have enormous barriers and hurdles, but the rewards can be tremendous. Unfortunately money is a requisite. So we need more results to take place, and they *can* happen, and they *will* happen, if we all work as a team."

The alleged *team* is silent. Cleo's former compatriot and accomplice is nodding slightly, having been subdued by this saccharine interloper. Starting today Cleo's a team of one. Not a partner, not a girlfriend, but the type of woman Windy wants, the kind with incentives that will also intensify a vigorous sexual drive — adding peril or heightened thrill. And starting now, Cleo's deliberate objective is to take Bishop down, and take everyone he's duped down with him.

"So if you carry out your programming," Bishop says, "it'll *pay*. Okay?" He's standing and the chair rocks back suddenly, wooden runners grinding on gritty linoleum floor. "Otherwise it'll be back to simple basic care."

Here's where Teri would've mumbled something about the morning cows never even manage to give that much, and *that* would be the reason Bishop called the two of them back. Instead Teri is standing and moving, already at the door, and her hand already on the knob when Bishop releases the others with, "Do your programs," then immediately, "Cleo and Teri, go get one of your patients and come back here. I'm going to observe your programs again."

Somehow that freezes Teri, so Cleo, erupting up from the waterbed and striding for the door, actually beats her into the hall, almost stepping on Danny who's on his back using his good hand to spin one wheel of his scooterboard. His delighted shrieks follow Cleo down the hall.

Jon needs to be changed and his shirt is damp with either sweat or milk from lunch — that's what it smells like but the curdled scent could just be him too — even though he's not supposed to have milk because it makes him congested. The kitchen makes a mistake with his diet and the cow doing lunch is too lazy to get him another drink.

With a clean shirt threaded over his rigid crossed arms, a clean stiffly starched diaper forced between his rusted-in-place legs, the dressing on his bedsore changed and another new dressing in her smock pocket, Cleo wraps Jon in a sheet and carries him back to the therapy room, kicks the door open, but only Teri is inside, with Danny — no longer on the scooterboard — his braces unlocked, patting his own reflection in the full length wall mirror. Teri's in the rocking chair reading a chart. Cleo places Jon on the waterbed, then reclines beside him.

"Nothing like a little therapy to make the day's work more relaxing," Cleo sing-songs, which could've been either commiserating or snide, depending on whether Teri is rereading Danny's program to see if she missed anything that could actually make it work, or reading a magazine hidden inside the metal cover.

A knock on the door. Danny turns, saying "*I-der!*" Cleo props herself up on her elbows. Teri clutches the chart to her chest and stands. Of course it's Bishop, the namby-pamby knocking as though they have a right to privacy. No one moves, except Danny, crawling to clutch Bishop's pants, to pat his leg, grinning with his tongue between his teeth. "Oh, I forgot his chair." Teri brushes past Bishop, still holding the chart.

It's been long enough since Cleo changed position that the waterbed has completely stopped moving. Bishop looks at her. "Be sure you get your oscillation stimulation." God, how many times does he use the same so-called *joke?*

"I *will.*"

For a second his powder-blue eyes actually ice, normal color nearly comes to his face. But he breaks his gaze away from Cleo and opens his notebook, turning pages.

Cleo lays the ingredients for another clean dressing — gauze, alcohol, medicated powder — in a line on the floor, then slowly begins to remove the dressing she'd just put on in Jon's room three minutes ago.

"Are you going to do his program?"

"This is more important right now."

Jon groans, but Cleo hasn't yet touched the wound with alcohol, it's some other groan. Gas, or maybe he's thirsty, she'll never know, but from the table she gets a cup with plastic lid and drinking spout — like a hard nipple — and trickles some water into his mouth, using the sheet to catch the surplus that dribbles from the corners of his lips, then patting his cheeks dry with a clean diaper she always keeps slung over one shoulder.

"Know how I give him a shower?" Cleo says brightly. "I can't bend him to get him into the shower chair, so I have to balance him across the two arms." A chill on her spine — exhilarating to actually sound so cruel.

"Let's see you do his therapy programs."

"With pleasure."

So she has Jon in a beanbag chair, his body in the usual position but at least supported so his head, still turned 90 degrees to his right, is higher than his feet. Bishop, at Jon's feet, lowers himself, bending his knees and balancing on the balls of his Hush Puppies. Cleo kneels on Jon's left, shaking the rattle, alternating it with a string of Christmas bells — not continuous rattling but short pops of sound, ten in succession, then silence, then ten more. There's no question she's read the program, knows exactly what it prescribes and why this is the correct technique.

Jon's mouth opens and closes, his eyes blink, nearly flutter, and the eyeballs roll toward Cleo, roll so far virtually only the yellowish whites of his eyes are visible. Then with a tiny jolt that even seems to cause a tremor in the sheet covering his feet, Jon's head moves, it turns, a little, almost to midline, half-way there. But Cleo also watches one skinny, stiff arm rise and vibrate before it falls back across his chest.

"Great! great, Jonny! Oh, Cleo, chart this right away!"

"*Chart* it?"

"Of course, why wouldn't you, he turned toward the sound didn't he?"

"You *know* he didn't. He's deaf —"

"Chart it. This is really great. You know the assessors are considering partial funding as an alternative to *de*funding, and Jon was on the cusp, they were going to take him off program-ming if he didn't show improvement."

"But —"

"Just multiply that by every child who shows even slight progress."

Cleo stands, still holding the rattle, Jon gasping audibly between them. "He hasn't improved, he —"

"Make note in his chart that he turned toward a sound, or I'll do it for you."

"You *know* he didn't."

"He moved. Period. Chart it." He's holding the chart, offering it toward her. The plastic balls inside the rattle chatter again when Cleo snatches the chart from him.

She has seen it before, seen it many times. It was a sei-zure. His body arched and his muscles jerked. She's supposed to go get the nurse immediately. Now it becomes *good* news because it was during his scheduled therapy hour, during his five tries. The same sort of involuntary spasm could've caused her to bash Bishop in the face. Or would have been the *only* way she would've been able to snatch the cigarette from Windy's mouth. Not among her normal aptitudes.

11.

Not a truce but a cease fire w/o any negotiating a window during a war when the 2 sides resume previous relations. Teri & Cleo in bed at night in the hush after midnight in a ticking house w/ humming refrigerator & buzzing porch light. Each in her own bed as usual then Cleo's at Teri's door w/ a pillow under 1 arm wearing sweatpants & sweatshirt & socks & says "Let's conserve heat" even though it never gets below 40 even in January. Cleo didn't go out as usual tonight was home all evening in her room w/ no radio no ring of her separate private telephone no creak of her bedsprings during abdominal crunches no thump of her barbell on the floor.

Teri hasn't even answered about the conserving heat suggestion but Cleo throws her pillow to the spot beside Teri's head & crawls onto the bed then just falls to her stomach head turned away from Teri. Add Cleo's breathing to the sounds made by the sighing weary house cooling off following another

12/hr day under the sun. Searching for even the kind of sleep that exhausts Teri counts sheep by mentally putting Danny's braces on & taking them off putting them on & taking them off pinning him under her body while 1 hand tickles his armpit her other hand strains w/ the pressure it takes to slide the lock across the metal joint & the leather creaks echoing the actual groaning stretch of his tendons & Danny's giggling eyes pop in surprise in that last second it takes to snap the braces straight. Now tonight the braces going on & coming off are also meant to lock her mind from its determination to try to remember what *did* happen the night when Sharon was conceived & was the patriarchal relative even *partially* correct?

The bed joggles b/c Cleo is doing something w/ her body like bouncing her hips but leaving her head on the pillow then she stops & she's face down in the pillow. "My fantasy" — Cleo's voice is thick like it's coming from under or inside the pillow — "is to seduce Bishop in the therapy room, *totally* turn him on, get him hot and naked, then tie him up and tell him I'm going to get something, like a French tickler — no that's a cliché — anyway leave and not come back, just wait and let someone else eventually go in there and find him."

No it's not compassion for Bishop that pings her guts it's b/c of how many people could've walked in to see *her* naked on a bed w/ limbs akimbo displaying wherefore the male had just finished depositing his sperm her 1st last & only college party & she wasn't even in college. But what did it matter she doesn't remember & apparently *he's* convinced & convinced the girl too that he swept her up a velvet staircase w/ sonorous violins playing & candles flickering w/ the scent of sandalwood & violets & mint which she loves the smell of in 1 of the yards she maintains she cuts the leaves & crushes them under her nose but how would *he* know her favorite scent or anything else considering that the day he followed her to the ob/gyn & cornered her afterwards to say he'd heard she was pregnant — demanding to know if it were true & what she was going to do — he didn't even know her name & had to *ask*.

"But I *will* take him down somehow" Cleo says as though Teri has argued w/ her humiliation fantasy. "It's such a goddamn Catch-22, *god* why can't I stop talking in flimsy clichés, anyway the sweetness-and-light optimism is sickening enough, but it's so phony at the same time, which is *worse* — if a seizure or spasm *looks* like a result of therapy, it's OK with him because the dumbass assessor will green-light the program, give more money, let the therapists keep their jobs, so they'll write *more* programs and we'll do *more* therapy looking for *more* phony results so we can get *more* money next year and the year after, yada-yada-yada."

She's right look how they make Danny cry & scream & contort in the hi-tech braces meant to straighten his tendons for *what* he'll never walk. Not Catch-22 just dead-end just for nothing just stupid uselessness like dialing the phone like trying to explain something she doesn't even remember & what if she suddenly *did* remember & what if what *really* happened makes her look worse instead of better? But she has to try & here's what she's got: As far back as she can remember it seems she's been working at the hospital but way back before Sharon now Shannon grew inside her then was born Teri lived w/ a roommate in an apt. & the roommate whose name escapes her did go to college & suggested Teri could pass as a freshman & get into the party not that they checked passports at the door. She doesn't remember thinking *he's cute* or hoping-&-praying she'd get asked to dance as she'd done in high school but somewhere somehow someone probably the other half of her child's DNA offered her a drink blacking out the next hour or 2 or 3 who knows. If she tries to recall her cynical brain colors in conceivable fine points she's not sure actually happened like the part about people standing in line & moving slowly past the room's doorway like a roped-off museum diorama titled *missionary position* & later *girl after intercourse* or even *girl impregnated* although they couldn't know at the time. Which is why she doesn't often actually never tries to remember. But now remembering might be her only chance to get Sharon back or even talk to her again to someday be able to say she's someone's mother not just someone's progenitor or rent-a-uterus or cow. So since yesterday she's been trying to prepare a recitation of the conception to the best of her recollection but tonight found out the number's been changed & there's no new number.

Twelve.

Is it possible she's as pathetically needy as Windy thinks she is? Is that why she's dragged her sorry butt from her own room into moribund Teri's?

Cleo had been home since right after work, the whole monotonous evening, and she sure wasn't going to be able to *sleep* at nine or nine-thirty — god knows what she would do all morning if she *did* go to sleep early and wake up at what, seven or eight? Take a skydiving lesson or buy a motorcycle, how about hijack a commuter train, show Windy how shallow she isn't? Yeah, it was at the moment when she'd realized that the moronic notion to hijack a commuter train actually meant commandeering a vehicle that *only* went back and forth between two destinations with no *possible* chance of variation — like where would she even have *taken* the damn thing — that's when she'd tucked her pillow under one arm and shuffled next door, like a kid having a bad dream, still half asleep until all the way to mommy's room, except it's not mommy's bed she's in — and it's sure not Windy's either — it's Teri lying next to Cleo, and she hasn't moved, not a flicker, not a shudder, not a flinch, not a sigh, since Cleo's been here.

"Hey," she tries again, like a kid talking to her stuffed animals, "did Bishop have the audacity to offer you a spot on day shift? I'd've said to shove the a.m. up his ass, and take all the piggy cows with it." Usually a unifying topic, and anyway why should they be adversaries anymore, Teri sure doesn't *seem* like she's still letting Bishop hand-feed her his light-at-the-end-of-the-rainbow trip — god-almighty, *another* cliché. But, anyway, it's the best way Cleo can muster to pass Teri an olive branch or white rose or whatever the hell means forget the spat, we're still in this shitty soup together.

Teri suddenly takes a deep breath, then has to clear her throat to answer, and says, "I'm considering taking it."

"*Why?*" Cleo jerks her body in one motion from prone to her knees. "God, Teri, it would be such torture, talk about slamming yourself into a brick wall, can you imagine, you'd be the only one washing your kids, changing diapers, checking their charts to see who's constipated then giving enemas, I can't believe you'd want to actually witness what those cows do or *don't* do ...."

Teri, on her back, still just gazes directly upward, stupefied like she's stoned. "Maybe it would be better for the kids to have one decent aide on mornings."

"Yeah, but ... isn't it futile enough on *our* shift? At least we're together — and we can feel like we're undoing some of their sloppiness. Imagine being one of *them*."

"I wouldn't *be* one of them," Teri's voice even more flat than her usual monotone. "My kids would be clean and fed for eight hours, and hopefully the new p.m. aide would keep them that way another four. Maybe I'll volunteer for nights too. Maybe I'll work sixteen hours a day seven days a week. I'll trust you to make sure my diapers are changed and beds are made from four to eight while I sleep."

"Now I know you're just being weird. It's Bishop, isn't it — that's what's changed you?"

"No."

"Yes it is. He needs to take it in the balls. Maybe *you* should seduce him then leave him high and dry, so to speak."

Finally Teri's head turns, but slowly, like a hydraulic machine, and she looks at Cleo and says, "Haven't you noticed? I'm an unresponsive zombie."

13.

A dream a dream *only* a dream her brain keeps repeating while it goes ahead anyway & takes her through the hallucination she doesn't even have to leave the bed. She must've fallen asleep somewhere along the line & now dreams she wakes still on her back stiff & heavy like all the blood has pooled around her spine & the sperm donor is standing beside the bed w/ an erection pointing at her face between her eyes & this time it's Bishop. Isn't this really Cleo's fault & all because of her silly humiliation fantasy or is this 1 of the scenarios Teri's distorted brain has conjured during 1 of the times she's tried or tried *not* to remember what really happened? He has 1 knee on the mattress beside her face & if he lifts the other leg to swing the other knee onto the bed on the other side of her head the engorged organ will be directed directly toward her mouth but that won't get her pregnant. Perhaps Teri has just recently been pushed backwards onto the bed & he's frozen at the moment of following

her but w/o surprise she watches Cleo's arm come from behind
& circle his throat her other hand appears also from behind
but down lower & places a knife against the base of his erect
penis. & through the whole slow-motion thing which actually
repeats several times Teri never moves. What *is* it Teri inadvert-
ently showed or even tried to teach her daughter pertaining to
her judgment or opinion of adult male *Homo sapiens*? She can't
remember did she ever say the word *Dad* to Sharon or was it
always *go pack your things the sperm donor's coming to pick
you up?*

Fourteen.

She never knew it would be so difficult to wake up in the morning beside someone else, to then have to escape into her own
room without disturbing or notifying the bulge remaining in
the blankets. Like a thief, a cat burglar who steals only a pillow, Cleo slips from the bed at dawn, moments before Teri's
alarm will go off. In fact, the clock begins its cybernetic beep-
ing almost exactly as soon as Cleo gets into her own room, like
a detector in a department or music store, sounding as she passes
through the doorway.

Due to their agreement, based on Teri's morning garden-
ing route, Teri always showers first. Cleo usually never hears
her — a late night, an exhausting one, morning sleep is often
the best. The spattering in the bathroom sounds like chicken
frying. There, let Windy call *that* a cliché.

The worst thing about today is tomorrow's Saturday. She's
never spent a weekend completely at home, doesn't even know

what Teri does, maybe vacuums, dusts, does Danny's laundry — she certainly doesn't go on dates or bring lovers home or talk to friends on the phone or go shopping. There aren't a lot of books around, no computer for chat-rooms or e-mail, the apartment's not *that* clean, and Cleo's never smelled gourmet lasagna or Thai chicken lingering in the air like she often can at Windy's.

Doing the exercising she skipped last night — decides half-way through to make it a double routine — allows Cleo a few hours sleep around noon. Then walks to work, will take a ride home in Teri's rattletrap Datsun that's held together with Band-Aids. It's the extent of her life now, she may as well accept it.

There are flowers at the nursing station. No one sends flowers to these patients, and seldom to an a.m. cow or nurse — it can and usually does only mean one thing.

Teri's already here, waiting with her wheeled tray-table for the afternoon laundry cart to arrive, her back against the high counter of the station, arms crossed, one grass-stained tennis shoe on the wheel base of her table, rolling it slightly back and forth. The flowers right behind her head. She doesn't watch Cleo approach, but does look when Cleo is finally there.

"Which one?" Cleo asks.

"Jon."

"I guess he moved toward the sound again."

As though she understands, which of course she couldn't because she wasn't there, Teri doesn't even raise her eyebrows or crinkle her eyes in question. She says, "You can't even go start to do your rooms. Bishop's in there."

"Shook?"

Teri nods, no she doesn't — it's her minuscule smile that seems like a nod. "Probably his first time."

"Let's go look."

"Why?"

"Let's just go."

Teri's footsteps are thumping behind Cleo. On the way down the hall they pass Danny's wheelchair, empty, his braces standing upright on the seat. Ordinarily, Cleo knows, when Teri arrives at work and finds Danny hasn't been braced, she'll do it first thing — changes his diaper and affixes the braces and amuses him until he stops screaming, even if it means missing first dibs at the laundry cart when it shows up.

A red ball rolls gently out the doorway of the therapy room, two rooms past Jon's room, and Cleo hears Danny say "buh!" then, clambering with forearms and bare legs, Danny crawls from the linoleum to the carpet, wearing only a diaper, a clean one, white baby undershirt, and his old white moccasins, just soft slippers to protect the tops of his feet from rugburn. So Teri *did* get here in time to tend to him.

Then they're in the doorway of Jon's room, staring in, as they had that other day, his birthday. Jon's bed is stripped. Piled on the shiny grey plastic mattress are all his possessions from deep in the closet: expensive clothes that were always miles too big, an Easter basket and stuffed purple bunny, a Halloween costume — a clown. The same block of yellow sun is now framing Bishop who stands at the foot of the bed holding his imperishable notebook, looking down at it, perhaps frozen in a permanent posture of figuring out a new therapy program for Jon, or maybe deciding how *this* can be charted as improvement. His eyelids are thin and blue. If he was horizontal instead of standing upright, it could've been *him* the flowers were for.

Not delicately, Cleo removes Jon's positioning graph from the door, leaving the four corners taped where they were. Bishop still doesn't move. "Hey," she lets her voice tear into the fuzzy yellow light, "if the assessors grant the money to continue his programs, do you still get to keep it?"

He looks up — but turns his back. The ball taps the backs of Cleo's ankles, but she barely notices, and has no idea what Teri's doing — probably staring slack-jawed as she had the other time there was an unthinkable scene in this room. Cleo steps forward, as though ushered into the room by the ball. "What's the matter, can't you turn toward the source of the sound?" Danny's palm smacks the bare floor somewhere behind her, and he makes his kissing sound. "Or will it take a seizure to make *you* look at me too?"

Bishop turns, his pale eyes crystal ice, frozen dead suns, "That's enough."

"*Is* it? Is it *ever* enough? There can *never* be enough therapy for blind, deaf kids with premature rigor mortis."

Bishop moves like a slow-moving monster lizard, his face grey, almost blue. "Despite what you may think, there *is* a reason to run the programs."

As he passes her, following his ball, Danny pats Cleo's ankle, then her foot, kisses air again. Where the hell is Teri? Why doesn't she say anything?

"You dare to presume what they *need*," Cleo hisses, "how the hell do you know what it felt like to *him* to have his corroded joints forced to move, to have his tongue jammed down and a spoon wedged between his clenched teeth, to not be able to get any liquid down his spastic throat, and when he has a goddamn seizure, *you* made me ignore it, chart it as progress, so I couldn't even tell the nurse. It's probably our fault he's dead. How's *that* feel, Mr. Asshole-improve-their-lives-with-therapy?"

Lying on the floor between Bishop and Cleo, his arm raised, about to bat the ball, Danny suddenly rolls to his back, the ripe, magnified eyes of a kid just before bawling. The hand that had been prepared to swipe at the ball is still raised, but now above his face as though blocking sun from his eyes. Meanwhile Bishop is aghast, but before he can react with whatever he's bound to do — maybe even cock a fist to hit someone, most likely Cleo — Cleo's smock is grabbed, yanked; without warning Cleo is stumbling sideways, pushed out of the way by *Teri*, storming the room. Cleo's shoulder and hip hit the closet damn close to Bishop, but she averts him and holds herself upright on the tray table. Teri is hoisting Danny by the armpits, clutches him across her body like a gun and heads out the door, biting off one sentence, "*He's* not putting up with any more of this shit either."

By the time Cleo gets into the hall — bumbling, again almost falling over the tray table — Teri's nearly to the door at the far end of the ward, taking six-foot strides, Danny's face looking back over her shoulder, his prior momentary alarm already turned to chortling, one of Teri's hands cupped on the back of his soft blond head.

"*Wait!*" That's not Bishop — it's *Cleo*. And she's running to get to the door before it closes behind the two departing figures, fused silhouettes in the glaring light of the glass entrance.

15.

Now what 1st go home then think. Somewhere there's an old permission slip procured from someone in authority allowing Teri to take Danny on brief field trips to a park to a shopping mall to places that excite him sometimes beyond even *his* ability to express glee — will that protect her from charges of something maybe kidnapping now? But no unanswered question is stopping her swift advance across the hot glaring parking lot someone flapping at her heels & doesn't see until pulling open the door to the back seat that it's Cleo opening the other side & leaning in to liberate the other half of the back seat seatbelt for Danny.

Now what at home they've set him on the floor not even a suitable chair to put him in & even if there were he'd need some kind of restraint to not only keep him there but to help him stay balanced his legs not strong enough to anchor him in a chair even his wheelchair had a seatbelt. No diapers no appropriate food not even a toy so Teri once again gets her keys & purse tells Cleo to watch him & goes to the mini-mart everything sky high but all in 1 place there'll be canned beans disposable diapers & rubber balls.

Now what's she going to do w/ him can't afford to move would have to move far maybe even out of state & isn't there some law against taking a child across state lines *hey* isn't that what the sperm factory did w/ the child that was hers so is this tit for tat? But she hasn't taken this boy from anyone who cared if he ever walks or talks or figures out what the potty training seat is all about & that his own b.m. isn't Play-Doh but down deep could that be what drew her to him in the 1st place was not his potential of which there isn't any but his perpetual infancy everlasting babe never able to make a decision about who to live w/ who he prefers & most of all 1 thing for certain he'll not be growing up to be a *man*. So pleased she'd been — if *pleased* could describe any of her attitudes having a baby w/o being asked — but some despondency defused anyway b/c Sharon turned out a girl & Teri was glad she was a girl b/c she'd never be like some sort of rooting animal probing for a place to deposit secretions produced by glands. Another fragment of evidence of what a sick poor excuse for a mother she was or *is* if you also count Danny.

Why not count Danny since now he's crawling around her living room all roughly 8 x 8 of floor space between 2nd-hand practically abrasive sofa & simulated woodgrain TV w/ colors ranging from muted brown to greyish green & the battle-scarred coffee table in the middle acting now as bumpers in a big billiard game knocking the rubber ball askew as Danny bats it & chases & Teri & Cleo stand staring — Cleo in the doorway to the bedrooms & Teri in the passageway to the kitchen. When the phone rings all 3 petrify — well Cleo & Teri are already fossilized but now even Danny stops as though *he's* expecting a call his Boy Scout leader canceling a campout or football coach scheduling practice but when the machine clicks on the caller hangs up which releases Cleo from being her own marble likeness & she says "What're we going to do now?"

"I don't know."

"We can't stay *here*, this's the first place they'll come looking. What can we say? You don't grab a kid out of a hospital and drive him home by *accident*."

"Well … were you counting on that hospital as your career for life?"

"I … Who thinks that far ahead?"

"I obviously can't think ten *minutes* ahead."

"Maybe …" Cleo taps the nail of her little finger against her teeth & she sort of has to snarl to expose the teeth so the nail can tap there. "We can take him to Windy's and hide him there. Even my parents don't know where Windy lives or they'd've given her an earful — they think I quit school because of her."

Of course when a kid does something dumb parents go screaming isn't it supposed to be some sort of instinct not something you have to be *told*? "Did you?"

Cleo pauses while Danny shrieks his eyes ardent & hot on the ball that due to no selection is neon green & purple paisley dizzying as it rolls. Then Cleo says "I made my own choices."

"I wonder if *I* did."

"C'mon, we don't have time to stand here having a heart-to-heart. Let's get this stuff together and take him over to Windy's."

"*Then* what, go back to work and say, WHAT *kid we just ran out the door with?*"

Cleo stops the ball with 1 foot & it's like Teri & Cleo are the pockets in this pool table & he finally got the ball into 1 so he screeches w/ jubilation rolls to his back pats his tummy w/ the good hand saying *buh buh buh*. "At least it gives us time to *think*."

"Okay, get the diapers, c'mon Danny, another car ride."

Still wearing smocks & nurse shoes w/ their jeans the canned beans fit in a smock pocket Teri & Cleo clamber back to the car like parents lugging armloads of kid-gear to the beach ball under 1 arm squiggling kid under the other Cleo grabbing cookies from the cupboard w/ diapers dangling by the plastic handle spiraling when her knee hits the soft package winding the handle up tight around her hand.

This Windy might as well live on another planet but it's only 2 miles a condo complex w/ private outdoor front doors but communal lawn & meandering sidewalk between identical bushes trimmed into balls on sticks & some trees tall Popsicle Cyprus no eucalyptus they shed leaves & god forbid someone have to rake it wouldn't be the residents anyway the gardeners are a *crew* who probably also tend the pool & sauna & hot tub do they even *allow* kids? There's no sign.

Teri stops on the zigzagging sidewalk 1 hip jutting way out to 1 side & Danny rides there a fistful of her shirt in his good hand behind her neck the weak hand a half-fist w/ arm extended palm-forward waving waving waving hello to no one or perhaps the guy w/ the leaf blower. Cleo ahead on the path turns around can't hear her but her mouth says "come on." So Teri's feet step forward again 1 foot then the other Danny's diaper making soft swishy sounds w/ each step — his version of creaking saddle leather this is the way the farmer rides. By the time Teri catches up to Cleo at the door of the unit where Cleo has been knocking the door is open & the woman who'd come into the hospital the other day is standing there who else did Teri expect she knew that was Windy.

"Hey didn't expect you" Windy says. "At least not so *soon*." Then it's obvious Windy sees Teri moving up behind w/ Danny who's kissing air & Windy's sassy sharp face suddenly bolts in fifty directions before reorganizing as a combination scowl & grimace. "Hey, what's going on, what's that gomer doing here?"

"Windy, please, we need some help." Cleo's voice weak & pleading in a way never heard at the hospital would've in fact made Cleo sick to hear any aide speaking this way to anyone xcept maybe while begging a stick-thin baby to eat. Danny's waving arm has lowered slowly like a hydraulic lever & his kissing stops while he stares at this strange creature standing on the porch blocking the doorway wearing large men's boxers & a sheer lacy teddy on top the red hair pushed up w/ a headband until it has become a nuclear explosion mushroom cloud or more like a short palm tree or 1 of those troll dolls.

"Windy, we'll explain everything, it's unbelievable what they're making us do, we sort of snapped, Teri snatched Danny and — "

"Then let Teri take Dannyboy somewhere else. What're you doing *here*?"

"No one'll think to look here, Windy, please, just while we think."

Teri lets the ball drop catches it with 1 foot after 1 bounce then holds it in place between her ankles & reaches behind her neck to work Danny's fist loose from her shirt so she can shift

him to her other hip his reactions slow enough that he's looking backwards for a few minutes no longer facing Windy's nasty
look of disgust which obviously means they won't be going
through this doorway any time soon so why has Cleo put the
diapers down on the top step why not just turn & leave when
it's clear you're not wanted? Danny's good hand now waving
in Teri's face & would be grabbing her glasses the way babies
always do if she wore glasses. Windy has little round wire John
Lennon glasses & could resemble John Lennon a little if she
tried & wouldn't look half bad but who tries to look like John
Lennon these days xcept maybe if Teri had idolized John Lennon
or even if she'd just pretended — or any other man like maybe
Einstein or Beethoven or maybe it would be more effective if it
were a man who was also *alive* — anyway Sharon might not've
come off w/ her assumption or more like a conclusion that Teri
is a manhater. 1 day maybe a week ago maybe longer Cleo had
said *being a dyke has nothing whatsoever to do with disliking*
MEN, *it just means my sexual attraction is for women. I don't*
hate Bishop because he's a MAN *but because he's a maggot.* Teri
could have said something similar had she thought of it on the
phone last night no 2 nights ago while she still had Sharon's
soft breath in her ear instead of the dial tone & since then an
electronic voice informing her the number has been changed
no new number.

"No" Windy says w/ what could only be called a corrupt
smile. "I don't want him here. You're welcome to stay but not
the nutcake."

"Windy, what if he were mine, wouldn't you want to protect him?"

"What part of *no* don't you understand?"

"That's such a cliché — "

"*Hey.*" Windy's voice snaps like gum popping in her mouth & Danny stops patting the top of Teri's hair w/ his sticky palm & stares cross-eyed w/ eyes so dark blue they're almost black. "You want cliché? Here's something for you to criticize little-miss-all-I-ever-wanted-was-to-earn-minimum-wage-in-a-shithole-hospital: *get him the fuck outta here.*" Then the repellent hateful smile again just a crack in her face & she's suddenly posing diagonally in her doorway 1 shoulder against the jamb feet crossed at the ankles 1 arm braced across the entry w/ palm flat against the edge of the open door. "Or how about this, since you so much don't want to be a cliché, you're welcome to stay, honey. I'd *love* it if you stayed. I'd sterilize you in a bubble bath and keep you all night if you want, and I *always* know what you want. But *only* if *she* takes Little Lord Braindead as far away as she can get him."

Teri can pick up the ball & leave or she can grab the diapers & go but not both & she'll have to decide so she's not moving which feels like she's nailed to the ground.

"Windy!" Cleo blows the name out like so much wind b/c there's nothing else to say but leave it to Cleo to think of something. "A relationship can't be tied to an ultimatum."

"Who said anything about a relationship? That's still up in the air, maybe, maybe not. The price to find out is lose the freak."

"It's okay, Cleo, we're going." Teri reaches for the diapers while the can of beans in her smock pocket swings forward & the ball starts a slow roll back down the sidewalk w/ Danny reaching for it leaning way over like a drooping plant saying "Buh!"

"No, she doesn't mean it."

"Don't I?" Windy straightens her posture & moves aside so the doorway is wide open showing off a foyer w/ spindly plain Quaker-style table decorated only w/ an ostrich egg held upright on an acrylic base. Could Windy be at someone else's home? "Come on in, Cleo. Let's spend an evening together. Like old times. Or maybe *new* times. How will you ever know unless you tell your friend to go ahead and take *it* away."

By now Teri has the diapers & Danny clutched together in front of her body in both arms like a bundle of laundry & he's still trying to dive headlong toward the surreptitiously escaping rubber ball but his blithe greeting for the ball has been replaced by a fretful whine. At her back the futile exchange proceeds 1 jabbered line answered by another Teri's not stopping to listen although recognizes Cleo's voice is hot wet & frantic. The voices are left behind as Teri follows the ball down the sidewalk planning no farther ahead than to tap the ball w/ her toe & herd it back out the gate to the car parked on the street but before she catches up to it hears a door slam & suddenly Cleo is in front of her picking up the ball rushing ahead cutting across the wall-to-wall lawn then out the gate & bounces the ball once twice 3 times on the sidewalk her head tipped back face toward the late afternoon still warm pale sky & her mouth is open matching Danny wail for wail.

Sixteen.

Teri drives, the two moronic broken-hearted crybabies sit together, the smaller on the larger's lap, and isn't that really the way it is, the bigger one indeed *is* the bigger baby, the bigger loser.

"We have to go home," Teri says, calmly, mildly, like a mother — a mother who'd thought it was a good idea to skip naptime and take two worn-out kids to the zoo. One's crying now because the pink, sweet and fluffy enchantment of cotton candy appeared then walked past and is gone forever. God, which one of them would *that* be?

Why the hell is she crying — well, not actually weeping anymore, but the same thing. Cleo thinks she might be moaning aloud but maybe it's not meant for anyone else to hear. Who is there to cry for or about *but* herself, her own simpering self, *she's* the one who decided, the one who actually murmured, after Teri had already turned and was leaving, "Windy, can I come back? After we take care of this, can I come back to-night?"

"Take care of it now," Windy had replied, "*You* choose — the retard or me."

"But we, like, *kidnapped* him, we could be in a shitload of trouble —"

"Call in your resignation and tell them where to find your friend. That's the deal if you want to *ever* come back. Turn her in."

Had she *thought* or was her choice an involuntary spasmodic twitch? Cleo's instinctive body must've known better than the rest of herself, the part that's sniveling but just has to accept that there *was* no choice, only one trajectory, only one brick wall to smash herself against, and hadn't she already landed on the same wall face-first just a few days ago?

They only live a couple miles from Windy, but Teri has turned onto the freeway.

"Where're you going?" Cleo mumbles. Danny makes one of those long trembly sighs that kids do when they're finished crying.

"His mother's."

"Couldn't you drop me off at home first? I ..."

"I know how hard that was for you."

"Yeah." Her own sigh doesn't seem to flush any of the garbage from her head. "How do you know where his mother lives?"

"I took her address from the back of his chart a long time ago. I always meant to go, to tell her how he's doing, to ask why she never visits, to let her know she should."

Danny, tears forgotten, reaches forward to slap the dashboard with his good hand. His weak hand imitates, but that arm, always cocked, can only extend halfway to the dash. "I drove by a few times but never had the nerve to knock," Teri finishes.

"God, how is *now* going to be different. *Nice to meet you, by the way I stole your kid*? Let's just *go*. Didn't she give up parental rights?"

"I'm not sure. The doctors are allowed to prescribe meds without her permission. Would that mean she wants nothing more to do with him or that she's allowing them to expedite treatment?"

"Shit, I don't know." The back of Danny's head periodically jerks backwards toward her face. She lets her neck tip over the back of the seat, waits for her eye sockets to fill and spill, but nothing comes. Her eyes are hot and dry, like if it was suddenly dark now, her eyes would be two glowing red lights. "I can't take much more, I need to ... can we go home?"

Danny starts to whimper again, arching and stretching, reaching indiscriminately in any direction his body will twist. "Don't you have anything he can hold?" Cleo asks, her own voice almost as much a whine.

"Look around. Garden tools?"

"No thanks, I'm not quite enough of a basket case to let him put out my eyes for me." But Cleo straightens, wipes her eyes on the back of Danny's shirt, then glances into the back seat and spots three gladiola stocks with somewhat wilted violet flowers. Holding Danny with one arm like a lifesaver, she reaches backwards and plucks one of the flowers with her fingertips. Danny's good hand immediately wraps around the flower stock, then he squeals softly, waving the flaccid purple petals as though it's a pinwheel.

After exiting the freeway, the neighborhood Teri is driving through is a middle-class tract with the usual lawns, bushes, sprinklers, and garage doors hiding bikes and headless dolls and neon plastic buckets and shovels and baby-sized basketball backboards. But the faded turquoise house Teri pulls up in front of is withering and decaying in a brown patch of weeds. "Oh no," Teri says, still gently. "I haven't been by here in a while. I was afraid this would eventually happen." Teri removes the flower from Danny's mouth. "I wasn't sure the address was current in the first place. Didn't even know if she was the one living here." The flower still in his fist, but apparently forgotten, Danny moans, his face puckers, he snivels the warning signs of another upheaval.

"I fucking can't believe this." Cleo is hot then cold, her heart pounding in her chest then thudding between her ears. "What time is it?"

"Judging from his fussing, it's after six. He needs to be fed." Teri puts the car into reverse and contorts herself to look over one shoulder so she can back up, even though there aren't any other cars parked beside the curb within fifty yards and she could've just pulled away going forward. "I wonder who's feeding our other kids?" When Cleo doesn't bother to respond, Teri answers herself, "the usual drill, of course, divide them up among the other groups. Dinner may be cold but they'll eat, the bed may not be changed but they'll sleep, and no one'll have time to think about therapy ...."

"What're you babbling about, are we going home *yet*?"

"All right, yes." Teri drives with one hand and uses the other to stroke Danny's hair from his forehead. "Can you give a kiss, baby?" He's still moaning, probably too tired to outright cry.

"God," Cleo says, "I wish I could whine and bawl and thrash around."

"*Aren't* you?" Teri's hand continues stroking Danny's forehead. "What can't you believe, anyway?"

"Huh?"

"You said you fucking can't believe this. What did you mean?"

"Isn't it *obvious*? I can't believe I've lost my girlfriend and apparently gave up my job, such as it was, to probably become a wanted fugitive, and I mostly fucking can't believe *you* must've actually thought you could just hand Danny over to his perfect-stranger mother and she'd say *thanks, why didn't I think of this years ago?!*"

When Teri crams on the brake all of a sudden, Cleo's forehead and nose crack into the back of Danny's skull. His unbroken whimpering becomes a steady scream.

"Dammit, Teri —"

"I'm sorry, baby."

Cleo takes her hands from her throbbing nose, but Teri's talking to Danny, dragging him from Cleo's lap to her own, cradling him across her body. His face is gathered into a little fist, eyes scrunched shut but mouth stretched wide, tiny tongue drawn way back, one of those silent baby-screams while he takes in air for the next vocal blast. But if Teri's good enough, the next peal will never come. Teri brushes his cheeks with her palm, rocks him, jiggles her knees, and she's singing something strange which Cleo finally recognizes as *My baby loves love, my baby loves lovin', he's got what it takes and he knows how to use it.*

"I'm sorry, Teri."

"No, you're right. He *has* a home. And now he won't have *us* there."

The rubber ball gets left in the car when they unload at home, but it doesn't seem to matter. Danny has beans and skim milk for supper, tied to a kitchen chair and shoved up to the table which comes up slightly higher than his armpits. He eats everything that's shoveled into his mouth, then plays with several cookies, making a gooey mess on the tabletop. Cleo sits watching Teri feed him. Every once in a while Teri hums or sings a line from that same oldie song. When Teri unties Danny and lifts him to lay him on the table, Cleo moves like a programmed machine, opens the diaper package, unfolds one, hands it to Teri and takes the wadded-up cloth diaper he'd worn since leaving the hospital, takes it into the bathroom to wrap it in the bath towel she'd used that morning. His teeth have been brushed and Teri has put Danny on the floor, in just diapers and white undershirt, ready for bed, and since the ball's not in sight he's not going to cry about it. From somewhere, Teri has produced a pink plastic doll with yellow hair which Danny holds by one leg and beats against the rug. She knows Teri saw the blinking light on the phone machine as soon as she did, when they first walked in the door, and they're both sitting here ignoring it. It couldn't or *wouldn't* be Windy, anyway … could it?

Reading her mind, but not very carefully, Teri — mopping the table with the same cloth she just used to wipe Danny's face — says, "Shall we listen to what he has to say?"

"He?"

"Bishop."

"Oh *him*."

"How soon we forget."

"Out of sight out of mind — I can match anyone cliché-for-cliché."

But Teri doesn't move, so it's Cleo who goes to the machine, heart thudding again, her joints hot and liquid, even though she knows it *can't* be Windy, won't be Windy — what if it *is* Windy, will she go back to her, will she go back *tonight*, does she have no more dignity than *that*? If it is Windy, she can prove she does. Prove to *who* — Teri? Why would Teri care, and how would Windy even know unless Cleo calls her back to *say* she won't come, but it's always more classy to not even call back. But it's not Windy.

Cleo is sitting on the floor beside the phone machine on an end table made of a wooden produce crate listening to Bishop and patting Danny's back while he pounds the doll's head on her thigh.

Miss Lightner, this is Frank Bishop. I, uh, just want to let you know we haven't called the authorities … yet. I know death affects people differently and I'll expect that by tomorrow you'll be ready to bring the child back and let him resume his life in the environment that's best suited for his requirements. I can't save your job, of course, but you can bring him back and there'll be no further action — if you bring him back in 24 hours. I'm confident you will because I'm confident you know that the right thing for the child is the facility that was designed around his needs.

Danny continues to beat the doll against Cleo's leg until the message is over, then when the answering machine resets with a series of beeps and clicks, that's when he cocks his head and listens. "Mum-muh," he says smiling to the doll, throwing it sidearm, then pivoting on his stomach to crawl after it.

"He doesn't even know his name," Teri says from the darkened corner where she's draped in the old armchair.

"The doll's name?"

"*Danny's* name. Bishop doesn't even know who we took."

"And he doesn't even care that I came with you."

17.

She could go back right now but he gave her 24 hours so what's the rush nothing'll be different in the morning & that way it won't be *her* shift but the AM cows who'll witness Teri delivering Danny to the 7 or 8 pairs of hands that'll be diapering him *p.r.n.* & feeding him *t.i.d.* from now on not to mention putting his braces on if they bother to follow the schedule he'll be happier if they don't & who'll care if they *do*?

Where he'll sleep is solved by Cleo once again joining Teri in Teri's bed & each adult careful to stay sleeping on her side facing away from the center where Danny is so that their 2 backs & shoulders become the crib rails which he can't climb over at least not without waking them. Instead of his own undershirt Teri decides to let him sleep in 1 of hers b/c she can pin the front & back bottom of the shirt together between his legs to make a baby sleeper & also pin the sides of the shirt to the outer sides of his diaper so in case he does have a b.m. in the night he won't be able to reach into the diaper not that he *always* does that. They change his diaper again barely wet & they don't have any lotion so Cleo gets her Oil of Olay & taps it on his groin saying "You'll stay young forever" then they exchange a look Cleo & Teri.

Before they can attempt to sleep on their sides facing away from Danny Teri lies the other way facing him & sings to him a different song "8 Days a Week" at least all the words she can remember something like *Ooo I miss your love babe 8 days a week*. Cleo — her back already to Danny remaining motionless like a crib rail should — sort of makes a sound a laugh or groan or both & Teri doesn't know very many more words than that so she just repeats them over & over & watches Danny's eyes close.

It's not easy to sleep & remain conscious of staying in the same position all night & of course he wakes them around 5 his normal routine hungry & wet & brimming w/ energy. Unfortunately it doesn't take long to undo & change a diaper & put his own shirt on him & find a pair of his jeans in their laundry not too dirty & certainly not wet. & doesn't take long to make hot cereal laced w/ honey which he's likely never had & maybe not even brown sugar Teri doesn't know what the kitchen gives the cows to feed for breakfast. Danny's hands don't even grab for the spoon nor pound the table top like they're suddenly paralyzed just sort of stiff. His mouth opens for the spoon as quickly as she can fill it always a good eater but never like this it must be the honey.

But too quickly there's nothing left to do & it's only 6 she sends Cleo to take a shower which eats a little more time then Teri can leave Danny w/ Cleo during her own shower & 1st messes around a little in the bathroom waiting for the water heater to fill but also killing more time. But killing time has its drawbacks too which Teri doesn't realize until Cleo says "he gets there early, sometimes by 8, the nurse told me" which means Teri won't be leaving Danny in his room w/ his toys for Bishop to discover when he comes in as though it was still yesterday instead Bishop will already be there wanting to play Frank & Earnest w/ anyone who's forced *p.r.n.* to interact w/ him.

Here's how to feel less humiliation — pretend instead she's handing off her own daughter Sharon to the fertilizer excuse me the man the *bio-dad* in front of the sperm's excuse me *his* relatives the uncles & cousins & grandma who by now all look on Teri as the mother-from-hell maybe they call her the egg donor. Whereas on the ward the cows won't know what's going on as usual & Bishop w/ his misplaced compassion & easily teary eyes can be made to consider Teri distraught over Jon's final seizure.

She tells Cleo she doesn't have to come along after all Bishop didn't mention her name on the phone & likely in all probability if later today Cleo shows up for work as usual at 4 no one will notice. Cleo doesn't answer very quiet this morning eyes pale not red or swollen & no whimpering nor snide remarks nor dramatic sighs nor grumbled asides. But when Teri hoists Danny to her hip & heads out the door Cleo doesn't close it behind her from the inside instead Cleo locks it from the outside w/ her key & follows Teri to the car. Nothing needs to be said Cleo puts the seatbelt around both herself & Danny on her lap & Teri drives the car. The gladiolas on the backseat she cut yesterday to bring in to the ward maybe the nurse's station or probably her own rooms a plastic hospital pitcher for a vase — they're dead now beyond wilted but Cleo takes another 1 & gives it to Danny to use like a magic wand touching everything he can w/ it.

Not only is Bishop already on the ward he's standing at the nurse's station facing the door practically watching a clock timing her return w/ the hostage. His slick slacks pulled up too far & his plaid shirt bunched together in front where his buckle covers the snap as though someone just recently grabbed both the shirt & the waistband of his slacks & gave him a good shake which he should probably get *p.r.n.* Lips pursed in self importance posing w/ 1 hand on the nurse's station counter like George Washington posing for a postage stamp saying "Thank you Miss Lightner" flicking 1 frail wrist twice a signal to the AM cow already sitting on her butt at the nurse's station as though her beds are all changed & kids all washed by 8:15.

"I'm sorry but your services are no longer needed here Miss Lighter. But I do appreciate that you regained some of your good sense. Perhaps this experience will help you learn something about yourself and you'll be able to continue to pursue a career in the health-care industry."

This chastisement won't be her worst humiliation because how can Teri pretend this pale noodle is her Sharon's genetic patrimony it's impossible so the real punishment is her last sight of Danny handed to the AM cow & Danny's face as he's carried away down the hall looking over the cow's shoulder above the cow's huge undulating ass — Teri's last view of him is just a little face like a 2nd head on the cow's body before she shifts him & carries him like a log sideways his eyes facing the rug & he's squealing & giggling like it's an amusement park ride & Teri's not even the one making it fun.

Beside Teri Cleo buckles as though she's collapsing down on the floor between Teri's feet & Bishop's is the dead gladiola stock Danny had brought into the hospital & Cleo is bending to pick it up. As Teri turns to leave all 5 of Cleo's fingers touch her arm stopping her & the 2 are suddenly facing each other a direct look in the eyes an exchanged wordless expression of coalition which used to occur at least *t.i.d.* always only on the ward but hasn't happened anywhere in a long while. & when Cleo does start to speak during her 1st few words she's still looking at Teri — "Mr. Bishop, if it's still available" — then releases Teri & moves to address him — "I'd like to have a chance for that full-time position on the morning shift."

Teri lets her feet carry her across the stained institutional carpet toward the glass door which at this time of morning doesn't throw that blinding block of light into the ward. The door is clear miraculously recently washed streak-free & outside Teri can see the eucalyptus trees bordering the parking lot need to be trimmed.

Eighteen.

When Cleo reported to Teri that she had managed to get herself assigned Teri's former group of kids, after a little redistribution due to Jon's death, Teri just nodded and turned away, and Cleo isn't too shallow to understand that was all Teri needed to hear of the basically unchanged comings, goings and daily routine at the hospital which haven't *resumed* but have, obviously, just persisted, maybe persevered — not that it would ever be something they would need to *discuss* anyway. Returning home in the late afternoon, eating dinner, watching TV, dropping into bed by 9, all felt too weird, too goddamn *quaint*, let alone having Teri there to witness it. They almost seemed to avoid each other in general chagrin, until Teri moved out and, alone, now the cycle is actually solace to Cleo, and it's how her heartbreak becomes nostalgic. And when it no longer feels pleasantly poignant to think of Windy, she hopes she'll have enough money saved to decide something, like maybe to go to nursing school.

19.

Teri never does attempt to get the hospital to subcontract her for tree-trimming in order to enable her to once a week peer through the glass door & maintain vigilance on Danny his life & growth. He's w/ Cleo 8/hrs a day & Sharon is w/ her father 24 a day & Teri doesn't have even the slightest twinge of guilt when she gets a new job as live-in nanny for a retarded handicapped girl landing the job *not* on the basis of having been a long-time employee of a state ward for severely mentally & physically incapacitated children but on the basis of 1st of all her willingness to maintain the property's landscaping & 2ndly her own personal experience of having had her own seriously handicapped — no call it disabled maybe impaired but hopefully not incurable — child.